THE MIGRAINE DIARIES

A NOVEL

THE MIGRAINE DIARIES

A NOVEL

ZACH POWERS

JACKLEG PRESS

jacklegpress.org

Published by JackLeg Press, 2026.
© 2026 Zachary J. Powers. All rights reserved.
Printed in the United States of America.

ISBN: 978-1-956907254

No part of this work may be reproduced or publicized in any form or by any means, electronic or mechanical, including photocopying, microfilm, recording, or by any information storage and retrieval system, without permission in writing from the publisher.

Library of Congress Control Number: 2024945782

Author Photo: Tiffany Lueong
Cover art: Christopher Kardambikis
Cover design: Emily Fussner Lam

For Stephanie, who is always very nice when I have a migraine.

"Your Migraine Diary is an important tool to help you and your doctor track your migraines, identify possible migraine triggers, and assess how well treatment is working. Try to make an entry each time you experience any migraine symptoms.

"Complete each entry as thoroughly as you can."

—migraine diary instructions

DIARY ONE

March 13

...

The phosphenes come instead of tears. Little stars superimposed over the world. Even that first time I know they aren't in the world, but in me. The idea of stars. This is what I think about to keep from crying.

At the edge of the ocean, Dolores stands barefoot with KJ's mom. They hold the urn between them. As if it takes two people. They're not doing anything, though. The problem with ceremonies is that they last way longer than anybody's comfortable with. KJ would hate this shit. He'd be interested in the phosphenes, though. He'd ask me so many questions about them.

KJ's mom looks enough like KJ from a distance to confuse me.

The wind on the beach should be all wind everywhere. Sunlight catches the tops of waves like a flock of doves. Like the phosphenes. I don't know what only I'm seeing versus what other people see, too.

Finally, Dolores lifts the urn's brass-looking lid, and KJ's mom dumps the ashes into the ocean. The wind whisks stray ashes away. I'm pretty sure this is illegal. There must be laws about the proper disposal of human remains. But it's not beach season yet, so the Tybee Island lifeguards aren't out. The Tybee Police are busy doling out tickets back in the parking lot. None of us mourners paid the meters.

KJ's mom taps the bottom of the urn like she's trying to get the last bit of tomato soup from a can.

Everyone is seriously crying now. Dolores and KJ's mom, ankle deep in the breakers. Hildie next to me. Blake and Chris. Lyn and Pru and Chuck over there. Usually when we're all together, it's by chance at a bar. There's something uncomfortable about this new gathering, our constellation on the beach.

Discomfort besides the obvious.

We follow Dolores and KJ's mom back to the wooden footbridge over the dunes. There's a pavilion at the midpoint, barely more than a gazebo, where we stop. KJ's friends take turns saying nice, if generic, things about him.

Blake, KJ's old roommate, steps to the center.

"Sometimes he was a pain in the ass," says Blake.

Laughing makes the stars brighter in my vision. A hundred novae.

Blake continues, "But there's a reason why we're all here, because he was always there for us."

I'm having trouble seeing Blake's face. I think the tears have finally come, but no, the side of his face has simply vanished. Carved out and hollow. I shake my head. A hurt grows behind my left eye. Shaking my head is a bad idea.

I imagine this is what KJ felt before the stroke that felled him. Logically, I know the chances of me having a stroke at the memorial for my friend who had a stroke are probably too slim to consider. I wonder if this is the way my body has chosen to show grief.

I'll later learn that *sympathetic* is never a word that adequately describes pain.

In my pocket, I carry a folded sheet of paper. The stock is heavy, the texture lush, ripped from an expensive sketchbook. It's the last item KJ gave me, days before he died. We were sitting on a blanket in a square on a sunny morning, the four of us. I was writing, him doodling. This was his final doodle, a cartoon corgi. He knew I love corgis. It stands on its stumpy hindlegs, forelegs like arms too short to be of any use. KJ used a Sharpie for the linework and a yellow highlighter for the color.

Blake's not talking anymore. He might've been done talking for hours. Time and space lose their meaning.

Faces turn to me. I should have words to say. I was the best friend.

All the faces are missing chunks. A monster took bites out of everybody's heads when I wasn't paying attention. KJ loved zombie movies. I can't stomach them.

The pain behind my eye solidifies. I shake my head to clear it. Everybody interprets that to mean I don't intend to speak. Which is accurate enough, I guess.

KJ's mom thanks us for coming. She cradles the empty urn like a football. Will she keep it? Use it as a vase?

People depart in groups of twos and threes. Their steps on the wood of the footbridge resound, timpanic. The ocean breeze is a jet engine. All activity hazes over. I hug so many people. I feel the squeeze on my skin but also in the spot behind my eye. Inside and outside get mixed up. I'm often accused of being a poor hugger.

The blindness abates. Everybody's head is back to normal except mine.

I follow Hildie to her car. She slides a parking ticket from under the windshield wiper. There's a cop cruiser at the far end of the parking lot, and she flips the cop off. Her finger is several times too long. I fear the cruiser is closer than it looks. Hildie always strides a misstep away from getting arrested.

Blake calls shotgun. I sit in back.

Where's Dolores? That's right, riding with her parents. It's an effort to remember where I am.

The pain has radiated down my neck. I calculate the ratio of ache to burn. The car lurches into gear. The pain surges in time with the bumps of the unpaved parking lot. I might puke. I've felt nauseated for several days, since I got the news, but the feeling is suddenly acute.

I lie across the back seat. I pull out KJ's drawing of the corgi and unfold it. The picture is alive, animated. It waves its stumpy legs. High comedy, this movement.

The corgi's mouth opens and closes, and I hear a voice. It's KJ. I turn my ear to the paper to make out what he's saying. I think it's "unfinished business," to which I whisper, "no shit."

What person dead at thirty-one doesn't leave behind a lengthy to-do list?

"Find it," says the corgi.

"Huh?" I ask.

"What?" asks Hildie from the driver's seat.

Lying down isn't helping, so I sit back up.

We exit the parking lot onto paved road. I can see the base of Tybee Lighthouse. Instead of a rising tower, I think of it as a spike pounded deep underground.

A left, a left, a right, a right. We're on Highway 80, heading back toward Savannah.

The pain in my head crescendos. Not moving is helping, but the movement of the car isn't. I fold the corgi and put him back in my pocket. He's still talking, but his voice is muffled. I close my eyes. A skeletal version of the road projects on the inside of my eyelids.

Hildie asks, "Did you say something earlier?"

"Nothing," I say.

That's the origin of the hurt. Or it's been there always, waiting for the worst moment to emerge. When the first doctor asks me to describe the hurt, what I should say is this: "I remember the throb in my head and the thrum of the road."

March 14
...

How do you write about a blur?

The hurt proper sets in after I get home from the beach. A pulsating, consuming pain behind my left eye. When I think it's as bad as possible, it worsens. Pain that numbs me to all else. I lie down and close my eyes and count breaths. Ibuprofen fails. Time and space morph into one looping spacetime.

I'm sure Death is coming. I'm hung up on the idea of dying, but I hope I can be forgiven for that. This pain, inflating inside my head, trying to pop out my eye and explode my skull, seems deadly. There's no good description of a deadly feeling. Anybody who feels death for real doesn't have time to jot down notes.

Maybe a smudge would be the best description, a blot of ink. I should write this diary with quill by candlelight.

The hurt on that first day rings new, but the more headaches I'll have, the more I'll doubt I haven't been in pain all along. As weird as the other symptoms are, it's pain that defines the experience, that defines me.

A stranger might point me out on the street and explain to a child, "That's the person with the hurt."

But I'm ahead of myself. This is a future I can't yet know.

All I do know on the morning after is that the hurt has drained me. My ass has been kicked from the inside. My muscles work at half-capacity. A sip of water turns my stomach. I'm aged by decades.

I lie on my couch and watch episodes of *Naruto* I know by heart. A dull ache settles like a bruise where my headache has been. It's nighttime and then bedtime and then morning. Space and time are broken.

March 15

I wake up and walk the forty yards to Gallery Espresso. Out my building's side door, through the cobblestone lane. In summer this stretch turns funky from the dumpsters. A quarter block on Bull Street, and I'm there.

Behind the register, Chris slops coffee for groggy tourists. Chris is always working. If I ever showed up and he was absent, I'd file a missing person report. He pours a house blend and hands it over without asking me to pay.

"Didn't see you yesterday," says Chris.

To be fair, I'm here about as much as he is.

"Had a headache," I say, the first of countless times I'll say this.

"Yeah, I finished off a bottle of bourbon when I got home after the beach. I don't know my last hangover like that."

I take my usual seat at the counter. There are six stools, facing back toward the rest of the shop, where clusters of vintage chairs surround squat tables. A wall of windows to the right overlooks Chippewa Square, full of tourists and live oaks. There used to be fewer tourists.

I panic at the sight of the empty stool at the end of the counter. KJ's stool. I can almost see him, a shadow in his shape. Or the cartoon corgi sitting there, speaking in KJ's voice.

The bruise-like ache in my head sneaks to the foreground. Not a headache, but the memory of one.

Chris squints at me, concerned. I must have winced.

"Jeezus," I say, "that seat."

"We should put a plaque there on the counter," he says. "Like the Jimmy Carter one at Pinkie's."

Chris refers to the plaque embedded in the bar at Pinkie Masters, marking the spot where the former president once stood to deliver a toast. We've all sipped beers off Jimmy Carter's embossed brass face.

Pinkie's is another place that KJ will haunt. His ghost is a blur, or a smudge. I want to knead the diffuse edges of the apparition back into solid lines.

In the square, a flock of small, dark birds lights from a live oak, shedding feathers.

Ahead, the windows face an old four-story townhouse that's now a law office. A pair of tourists pause to photo the house's fish-shaped downspouts. Farther to the left there's a British pub, complete with a red London phone booth out front. A man wearing a Savannah-branded sweatshirt poses by the booth for a selfie.

I startle at a hand on my back. Hildie's snuck up on me. How did I miss her entering? I'm facing straight at the door. She sits in her usual seat to my right. Chris brings her an espresso. How did he prepare it so quickly?

Hildie leans in, her shoulder bone poking into my shoulder muscle. I give her a one-armed hug. I'm often accused of being a poor hugger.

Hildie recently showered. Damp hair. A shampoo scent, bubblegummy. She got a haircut recently, too, an undercut, tips dyed teal. The tips shift color so often as to be symptomatic.

She tilts forward to look past me.

"His stool," she says.

I'm stuck in the turbulent point between normalcy on one side and novelty on the other.

"Chris suggested a plaque," I say.

"Like Jimmy Carter's," she says.

KJ, Dolores, Hildie, and I have sat in a row at this counter for years of mornings. Breakfast Club, we call it. We sit here and work on our creative projects, a couple writers and a couple artists, and then we disperse to day jobs.

"Do you remember," asks Hildie, "when we found out Dolores and KJ had been secretly dating?" She's still regarding KJ's empty seat.

"Have you seen her?" I ask.

"I called. She said her folks were smothering her, but at least she doesn't have to cook her own meals."

"I ate some toast yesterday."

Hildie flags down Chris. She flicks her thumb at me and says, "Get this dumbass a croissant."

"Thanks," I say.

Hildie straightens her posture and sets her hands on the counter. She inspects each hand in turn. Short nails, dried paint caught up in the cuticles.

"It feels weird sitting here," she says.

The hurt expands deep inside my head, deeper than seems possible, as if instead of a brain I have a wormhole, descending through space. The hurt comes from distant galaxies. I think about the *hurt* in *hurtle*.

"Will it stay feeling like this?" I ask.

"I hope so," says Hildie. "I hope it doesn't go back to feeling completely right. Because that'd be bad, wouldn't it?"

Her voice arrives from a great distance. I'm hurtling through the wormhole in my head, seeing where it takes me. To or away from. Or it's looping, and the journey leads back to the empty seat beside me.

Hildie nudges my arm. "You okay?"

I leave the wormhole. The sounds of the coffee shop and the smell of coffee and the sight of the worn wooden counter drift toward me. Ashes on a sea. I'm back in my seat again.

"My concept of bad has been greatly altered," I say.

"I like Chris's suggestion about the plaque," she says.

I nod, but I know we'll never follow through on the idea.

March 16
...

I meet Dolores and KJ's mom at KJ's apartment, half a duplex in midtown. I only now think of his tabby cat, Hobbes, and if he's OK, and who's been taking care of him. Hobbes runs up to Dolores and nuzzles her leg, so that last question, at least, seems answered.

The apartment itself is a cluttered, dusty mess. Little more than a storage unit. This is where KJ kept his stuff—a library of movies and comic books, a museum of action figures—while he mostly lived in Dolores's nicer place by the park. His lease was set to expire before the wedding.

I can hear in my head the joke he'd make about getting out of the lease early.

I pick up a DVD case from the coffee table in the living room. The title is in Japanese, probably bootleg. I don't recognize the movie, but that's the norm. KJ introduced me to all my favorite movies. I set the case down. Dust kicks up. A tiny, dusty explosion. I inhale the particles. The dull ache is still there in my head. Sometimes I don't even notice it anymore.

KJ's mom paces from corner to corner, looking at KJ's stuff as if it belongs to a stranger. Which I suppose is how it goes with parents and grown-up kids, except in those weird, extra-close families. At what point do our parents stop knowing us? I suspect it's earlier than one might assume.

KJ's mom adjusts a framed poster of the band They Might Be Giants, righting it. She runs a finger over the top of the frame, rubs the dust from her finger with her thumb.

She makes a scrunched expression I recognize from KJ's face.

Dolores bears trash bags and boxes. Dolores is on a mission. I admire the way she handles bad raps, finding an element within her control and controlling the hell out of it. Her fiancé is dead, her life damaged beyond repair, but here's a task that needs doing. She begins to sort objects according to her own private system.

I'm not sure why I'm here. I'm not sure what I have to offer. I've known KJ longer than anyone except his mom. I've shared more movies and comics and books with him than anyone except Dolores. But looking at these fragments of his life, I can't piece them together into the person he was.

It's his ashes all over again. Just dump the whole lot into the ocean and be done with it.

I know I should be here now for Dolores. I've known her nearly as long as I knew KJ. But our past closeness creates present distance. I'm inadequate to the task of comforting her and she knows me well enough to know it.

I check out other rooms. KJ's bed is made, but there are depressions along the sides where he sat.

A desiccated bar of soap rests atop the comically small sink in the bathroom. No shower curtain, only a liner.

The kitchen has the face of an ancient man, peeling veneer on the cabinets, the doors misaligned and drifting open. Silver light filters through the window in the door to the back porch.

KJ's office is both cleaner and messier than the rest of the apartment. Its surfaces are dustless, but sketchbooks and stray pieces of paper are flung all over. I struggle to step in free spaces on the floor. It looks like that scene in every spy movie where the spy discovers that their hotel room has been ransacked.

KJ did most of his work at the coffee shop, but he'd bring his sketches here to digitize them, performing whatever computer magic it was that turned them into finished illustrations. I move his mouse. The login screen pops up on the laptop.

Stars have returned to my vision, but I'm ignoring them. Fuck these stars. Instead, I think of snowflakes, which is better because those are closer.

The office shelves overflow with the books KJ used when he taught classes at the art college. I try to read the titles, but words aren't making sense. Letters go missing. The blind spot is back, but it's not how I would have imagined blindness. Parts of objects are invisible or smudged out, the parts I'd need to decipher them.

One bookcase is full of comics. The *Watchmen* graphic novel rests horizontal on a shelf, the *N* absent from the title. *WATCH ME*, it commands.

The spaces between the books pulsate. I look at a bare white wall and it fractures. I expect an earthquake, a reason the world is growing seams.

Dolores comes in. She speaks, but I don't quite hear. She selects a sketch from the floor, rough pencils of a rocket ship. Think Buck Rogers. Dolores drops the sketch. The room's mess upsets her, I know. KJ kept things straighter at her apartment.

Dolores's face is wrong. A cubist portrait, pieces broken off and rearranged, made abstract. The face of my friend, now the friend I've known the longest. I seek her eyes. I find one of them and focus there.

"You can take whatever," she says. "We're going to donate the rest, the comics and movies, to the college."

"He'd appreciate that," I say. I maybe say it. Rushing wind abrades my ears. There's a numb sensation at the tip of my tongue.

"I already have the stuff I want at home." She chokes the last word. Half her mouth is below her chin and the other half is up where an ear should be.

This is the first time Dolores and I have been alone together since KJ died. There's something I'm supposed to do. Reassemble her face, for example. The moment creeps. Spacetime is screwed again.

Maybe I can loop back and take KJ's place. Be the gone one. Already I'm barely here.

I keep it together enough to give Dolores a hug. Not a good one. So much practice recently and still so bad at it.

My fingertips tingle.

Dolores doesn't cry.

She steps back. Her face sorts itself out.

The tingle travels up my arms. The dull pain, the memory of the previous headache, solidifies. I'm traveling to the past. Pain and memory. Somewhere on KJ's shelves is the DVD of *Groundhog Day*.

"Take whatever you like," she repeats.

I follow her out to the living room where all KJ's shit has already been boxed. Trash bags heap by the door. What the hell is happening with time? KJ's mom seems older.

The hurt throbs hard and I gulp. It's the loud gulp of a cartoon. Think Scooby Doo. Dolores and KJ's mom look at me.

"You OK?" asked Dolores.

"Headache is all," I say.

"You should get out of here," she says. "We're almost done, anyway."

Have I helped? Was I there packing with them all along?

"Thanks," I say.

Before I leave, I claim KJ's big action figure of Galactus, the cosmic being from Marvel Comics, a full foot tall and with a button on the back you push for him to speak catchphrases. I push the button and Galactus's voice, both deep and puny at once, declares, "I hunger."

The sun outside overwhelms. There's not a single car on KJ's street, but I hear highway traffic. Each step entrenches the hurt. I think I'm dying. I drive home, anyway. I shouldn't be driving.

I know Dolores is there behind me. I know there's something I should do for her. Find it, the corgi told me. There's nothing to be found. The city blurs around me.

March 17
...

The hurt again lingers for hours. I'm bedridden. At its worst it leaves me gasping. I don't know that I've ever whimpered before but have now proved myself capable. I take a nonspecific number of ibuprofens. Finally, I fall asleep, and when I wake up, the hurt has faded back into a dull memory of itself.

It's 6am. There's already noise outside on the street. I realize it's St. Patrick's Day. Under normal circumstances no Savannahian could forget the holiday's approach. Our biggest event, love it or hate it. KJ loved it, despite his lack of Irishness.

My innards are wrung out. Did I eat last night? I gag at the thought of food, but it's not like I haven't been hungover before. Sometimes a gag is your body not knowing what's good for it. I throw on clothes and brush my teeth and ride the elevator down to the street.

Immediately, I encounter a person drunk on green beer. They slur me an "Erin go Bragh." Are they still up from last night or simply starting early?

My apartment building is in the center of the parade route. The parade passes by one block to the east at the beginning and one block to the west at the end.

Crews are setting up barricades. Families claim spots along the parade route with folding chairs. The lights of cop cars strobe in the early morning dark.

I go into the breakfast place next door. It's thankfully open through the hoopla, though they've truncated the menu to four items. I order a skillet with corned beef and hash on eggs on hash browns. I sip coffee.

The building used to be an auto shop. They raise the massive garage door while I sit there. Outside sounds come in.

I try to recall the lost hours. The hurt is no longer a blur. The hurt has substance, but that substance is subatomic. I lack the proper apparatus to view it. Microscopes or whatnot. Pain is a state of the particles that make up the atoms that make up me. Up quarks that are down and vice versa. My bosons, misaligned.

My food arrives. The corned beef and hash is the canned kind, but sometimes that's the taste I'm looking for.

I imagine a single particle and trace its track back to the Big Bang. I wonder if along the way had it been deflected just so much, I wouldn't be in pain now. The pain particle.

Time and space are bullshit.

I wander back to my apartment. I don't remember the details of eating, but the grease lodges heavy in my gut.

I follow the sounds of the parade. A marching band passes by playing the *Notre Dame Victory March*. Later, the same band passes by on the other side playing the same song.

A cannon fires. I assume the Shriners and their pirate ship float.

I've taped KJ's sketch of the corgi to the wall by the window over my desk.

I can't see the parade from here, but then I'm watching it. I'm sitting on the curb next to kids with shamrocks painted on their faces, and the corgi's there with me. He's not a real corgi, but the sketch blown up to nearly human size. He holds a beer can in his stumpy corgi paw. He sports a leprechaun's hat.

If I blink hard, I'm back in my apartment. The image returns. I'm outside at the parade with a person-sized dog.

"I like to think of beer as space dust," says the corgi in KJ's voice.

A troop of uniformed kids from the local military high school march by. Boys pretending to be men. Moms and aunts and girlfriends have left bright red lipstick marks all over their cheeks. Loving wounds.

"My beer was made by fucking *fusion*." The corgi draws out the final word and then laughs the way KJ did when he'd amused himself and couldn't care less if anyone else laughed along.

Each beat of the laugh upsets the sore spot in my head. I imagine my brain's atoms fissioning.

I get up, back in my apartment, and ride the elevator down to the street. I tunnel through revelers toward the parade route. I pick out a shady spot and watch.

Colonial Cemetery is across the street. Spectators climb the cemetery's wrought iron fence for a better view.

The Shriners vroom by in miniature dune buggies. Doughy, middle-aged men acting like kids.

I've never watched the parade alone before. I've never watched it sober.

Parades, as a concept, look silly on paper.

I stick it out until the end. Cops on horses trail the final float. I don't know whether the horses are the last part of the parade or the first thing to follow.

It feels important to figure that out.

My Personal History of Pain
Part I
...

I'll start with a simple pain in my ass.

This was a couple weeks ago. At Dolores's suggestion, we met up that morning in Whitfield Square instead of the coffee shop. The weather had turned warm. Not the start of spring, per se, but a preview.

Dolores and KJ spread a gingham picnic blanket on the sunny side of the square's gazebo, white-painted, octagonal, genteel. They'd brought coffee in a carafe and scones in a basket. Hildie showed up with champagne and OJ and flutes, actual glass, for mimosas. When I asked Dolores if I could bring anything, she declined. She knows me well enough to doubt my follow-through.

Everybody worked on their usual stuff, KJ and Hildie sketching, Dolores writing in a pocket-sized notebook. I hadn't thought to bring so much as a pen.

This is a memory of pain because my corner of the blanket overlapped a tangle of protruding roots from a nearby oak. No matter how I shifted, a root dug into me, some new, sharp angle. Even if I'd brought my notebook, I couldn't have gotten comfortable enough to write.

Across the square, a crew from the city shoveled pine bark from a pile on the sidewalk, spreading it around fresh plantings, little bushes that would need several more springs before they would count for anything. The pile of bark diminished by the shovelful.

A pair of old men sat on one of the benches, rickety aluminum walkers like scaffolding in front of them. They'd trekked through the crosswalk from the senior living tenement across the street, a line of impatient cars waiting, stealing jerky inches forward.

Now the roots dug into my hip. Now the back of my leg. I tried lying back to look up through the canopy of branches, but the roots found my spine immediately.

"You alright, bro?" asked KJ.

"Tree roots attacking my ass," I said.

Hildie scooted over and patted the space she'd made for me on the blanket.

My new spot was relatively rootless. The feeling of the hurt faded. So there had been one kind of pain to start, and another kind as it diminished. But to describe them precisely, I would have needed to make notes right away. I would have needed my notebook.

A woman walking a corgi entered the square. We always saw the pair around downtown. Sometimes they showed up in Pinkie's. The corgi was chill even on the busiest nights at the bar, sleeping beneath a stool, raising his head for pets from everybody. The corgi's name was Oliver, but I'd never thought to ask the woman hers.

I sensed KJ watching me watch the dog.

"What?" I asked.

"Why don't you get a dog?" asked KJ. He knew I loved corgis.

"Because I live in a 250-square-foot apartment."

"Why don't you move to a bigger apartment?"

"Because it's all I can afford downtown."

"Why don't you get a new job?"

This was the familiar pattern to our banter. Dolores and Hildie stopped working to watch. It was half performance, after all.

"Because," I said, "I already have the best-paying job in Savannah doing what I do, at least until my boss retires. Only other option would be to leave town."

"Don't do that, bro," said KJ. The bantering tone had seeped from his voice. He drew a few lines in his sketch pad, stopped, flipped to a blank page, and started something new.

"I've been thinking," he said, "about the randomness of how we all met, and how easily we could have ended up in different places. I mean, we all have regrets, right? The thing we might have maybe done that would have taken us somewhere else entirely. But I look at us here, this privileged little life in a pretty square, and I think we got it right. No, I won't ever draw Metamorpho for DC, but there are only a few people who get to do that. In exchange for this," he pointed all around with his Sharpie, "I'll make do with Metamorpho fan art."

"Selling like hotcakes at Comic-Con," I said.

Hildie nudged me with her elbow.

I have a habit of deflecting nice moments.

Dolores leaned over and kissed KJ's cheek. He kept drawing through all this. I was always impressed with how for him the act of drawing was separate from the act of thinking, the type of mastery where thought is redundant.

He capped the Sharpie and traded it out for a yellow highlighter, the cheap kind you buy in the office supply section at the grocery store. He started with broad strokes and then went around making smaller squiggles to fill in tight spots.

"Here," he said. He ripped the page out of his sketchbook and gave it to me. The paper was crenelated along the top from the torn spiral binding. The drawing showed a cartoon corgi, standing on its stumpy hind legs.

"The perfect dog," he said, "for your tiny-ass apartment."

I didn't know what to say. KJ always had a way of being sweet I couldn't comfortably reciprocate. Some sort of response felt necessary.

Everybody was looking at me. My friends. The old men on the bench. The workers across the square who'd finished shoveling pine bark and now leaned against the handles of their tools, smoking. I imagined faces staring out of the ornately framed windows of the old houses surrounding the square. I shifted under the weight of gazes.

Still, a reply wouldn't come.

A tree root poked my thigh, hard enough I'd find a faint bruise there three days later.

March 18

I return to my job today. It's been millennia since I was here. I'm surprised to see the same people I used to work with. Shouldn't we all be dead by now?

The TV station operates out of an antique building downtown. Brick, four stories, flanked by a 300-foot broadcast tower. My office, where I edit local TV commercials, is entombed in the building's most sunless depths. I sit at a massive desk, built back when video editing required multiple tape decks instead of a single laptop computer. The laptop plugs into twin monitors, the only sources of light in the room. There's a second edit station, but we haven't hired another editor since the last one quit ages ago.

Blake comes in to tell me he's finished the graphics for my morning edit. He doesn't need to tell me this. I'll find the files on the server. This is Blake's way of checking up on me.

It feels like more than coincidence that I work with KJ's old roommate, but it's not. Savannah is a miniscule city. Practically subatomic.

This morning's edit is for a local car dealer. Every month, we do a dozen commercials for the guy. He stands—frumpy, egg-shaped, long since bald—in front of a Ford F-150, dully reciting the latest deals. Every car on the lot is always marked down.

For some reason, the dealership's mascot is an emu. Each commercial ends with the same three-second video of an emu running in a field. The emu clip predates me, an artifact. It was shot in standard definition. It looks like shit on newer TVs.

Within the office, epic legends have sprung up about the emu's origins. As if any explanation would suffice.

I don't need to think about these commercials to complete them. I've edited several hundred versions before. The morning passes. I forgot to bring lunch, so I get Pop-Tarts from the vending machine. I pull up the next edit and start as I eat.

I can't quite focus. Not on my edit. Not on my food, such as it is. I rock in place. I stop rocking, but the images on my monitors keep moving. The video is paused, the motion not the sort there should be. My sense of depth shifts, like when Spielberg does that trick where he dollies the camera out while simultaneously zooming in. Flying forward, but not in a fun way.

The monitors are too bright to look at, so I shut them off. Complex patterns play across the dark. The world is kaleidoscopic. I count the sides of shapes. Jittery images wheel in front of me. I'm watching an old cartoon.

It's no surprise when the hurt returns. It's my emu, a predictable, inexplicable end.

I leave the office and walk home without telling my boss. No one will call me on it. No one can edit car commercials as quick as me.

The hurt skewers my brain with each step, getting worse, turning impossible. The walk takes days. The sun hangs idle in the sky. I pass a single townhouse for blocks. By the time I'm home and press the button for the elevator, tears leak from my eyes.

The hurt won't relent. It drags slow moments out to forever.

Hours and hours and hours.

That evening Hildie brings me a plain bagel from Gallery. Usually, I add cream cheese, but all I want is butter. Hildie scrounges some from my fridge. I'm surprised that it was in there. I don't dare ask her to check the expiration date. I'm not sure if butter expires.

The hurt is less but not gone.

Hildie sits next to me on the loveseat as my TV plays episodes of *Naruto* we both know by heart. She holds KJ's Galactus action figure in her lap like a pet.

She reaches up and touches the skin under my eye. We have the intimacy of old friends who've drunkenly seen each other naked.

"You look horrendous," she says.

"Nice of you to notice."

"Have you had headaches like this before?"

On TV, Naruto, the titular young ninja, is mastering a new ninjutsu, his face scrunched with exertion.

"How can I even answer that?" I say. "I've had headaches before. Maybe they were not-as-bad versions of what I'm having now. I haven't cataloged them." Talking flares the pain.

"Well, what are the headaches like?"

"It's like everything changes, looping back into itself, like the moment never ends."

I try to explain the alteration of space and time by gesturing at my bagel. Hildie leans over and takes a bite out of spacetime.

"Yes!" I declare. Because the hurt is also like a bite out of a bagel.

She chews and glances around my apartment. She points at the corgi drawing.

"One of KJ's?"

"The last one he gave me. That morning in the square. I realized I've lost so many of his drawings over the years. How many doodles on how many napkins did he give me?"

"You should frame it."

"I sort of like it unframed. It has more potential that way."

She takes another bite from my bagel, completely severing the circle. Bagel skin sticks to her front teeth. She probes at the residue with her tongue.

"I haven't seen Dolores since the beach," she says. "We should go out to dinner this weekend. Nothing fancy, just something normal."

"What even *is* normal anymore?"

Naruto masters the new ninja technique on TV. Hildie and I high-five.

"Your head is definitely not normal," she says. "You need to see a doctor."

"It's only stress," I say.

She gently taps my forehead with two fingers. "Go. See. A. Doctor." One tap for each word.

I promise her I will.

At some point I fall asleep. These headaches leave me exhausted, guts wrung out, body weighted with sand.

When I wake, Hildie's gone. She's left the final bite of bagel on a napkin where she sat.

March 19
...

The doctor can squeeze me in late the next morning, so I call in sick to work. I easily could have knocked out a few commercials before my appointment. The doctor's office is literally across the street from the TV station. But I'm wary of the illusion of falling through the computer monitors. I don't want to find out what's on the other side.

The doctor's lobby is cold and permeated with sick. I try not to imagine how much snot has dripped on all the surfaces. I look at the stacks of magazines longing to read one. I should have brought a book.

I've been to this doctor before, so there's less paperwork than if I was new. But there's still paperwork. I have a chill. After a headache, I'm unwarm, my blood hesitant to flow at full strength. I consider piling all these forms on the floor and starting a fire.

I return the forms to the friendly receptionist. He always chats for a moment with the patients. I choose a new seat near the TV. *The Price Is Right* is playing without the sound. A contestant spins the big wheel. The wheel's motion triggers a sensation like carsickness. I look away.

A nurse calls my name and I pass into the secret back of the doctor's office.

I step on a scale. I step off. My butt crinkles the paper on the examination table. The nurse takes my vitals. She leaves. I sit for ages and learn all about the inner ear from a poster on the wall.

The doctor comes in and calls me *Mister*, a clear sign that doctors don't really know their patients. She asks what I'm in for today. I answer, the fourth time I've explained the headaches, first on the phone when I scheduled the appointment, then when I checked in, then to the nurse, and now to the doctor. She nods and adds notes that must resemble the notes made by the nurse. The doctor clicks her pen shut.

"What you describe," she says, "sounds like the symptoms of migraine with aura."

The word *aura* makes me think of the aurora borealis, which I've only ever seen in pictures.

"Have you had migraines before?" she asks.

"I've never had a headache that I've called a migraine."

"What about the visual hallucinations?"

"What is reality, anyway?"

She stares at me, unblinking.

"Not that I recall," I say.

There are more questions and a cursory exam that mostly involves the doctor shining a penlight in each of my eyes, but as soon as she said *migraine*, she seems indifferent. She's slipped me into the correct pigeonhole. A course of treatment unfolds before us.

"For now," she says, "keep taking ibuprofen for the pain. Take it at the first sign of symptoms. It's important to cut off a migraine attack as early as possible."

I latch on to the word *attack*.

"And keep a diary of your symptoms and what you were doing before a migraine starts. What you ate or drank, where you were, specific activities."

"I was at a funeral the first time," I say.

Her eyebrows raise, and she jots another note.

"We'll schedule a follow-up appointment in a few weeks. If the headaches go away, feel free to cancel. If they get worse, or you develop new symptoms, please contact us, and we'll see you sooner."

She gets up and offers the requisite pleasantries. The nurse returns shortly and sends me back to the front desk to make my co-pay.

On the walk home I ponder the word *attack*. I've never really had an enemy before, but now I expect one behind every blooming azalea bush. Every passing car a drive-by shooting. Evil ninjas lurk in the knobby branches of the live oaks.

But in the end, it's me attacking myself.

The exertion of walking aggravates the spot in my head where the migraine used to be. *Migraine. Attack.* Two words I'm not used to using.

The discomfort in my head is a precipice. I stand a step away from tumbling over the edge. Pain as a pit or a crater or a canyon.

I hear KJ's voice. Not a hallucination, but a memory. To be fair, a memory of a hallucination. "Find it," KJ-cum-corgi told me. Should one accept a quest from a hallucination? To be fair, I suspect most quests have similar origins. And most epiphanies and most religions.

And what does the version of KJ haunting my brain want me to find? Inasmuch as the KJ in my brain is actually my subconscious, what does my subconscious want me to find vis a vis KJ? What the fuck am I thinking about?

I do like the idea of a quest, though. Life has turned mysterious since KJ died, and all good mysteries crave unraveling. I go past my apartment and wander along with the downtown tourists. I try to see the city like they do. The low, old buildings, the ancient trees in all the squares, monuments, historical markers.

I'm looking for clues, I tell myself, but mainly I'm just walking.

March 20
...

Whenever I leave a doctor's office, I know how much I failed to say. I know that it's my failure to find the right words that will lead to a failure to find a cure. Virginia Woolf said, "let a sufferer try to describe a pain in his head to a doctor and language at once runs dry."

At least I know I'm not alone in my muteness.

March 22
...

I had a couple more migraines, but I didn't think to write about them. I don't remember what I was doing before they started or exactly how the aura progressed. I remember the hurt, of course, but not specifically. All I recall are flashes of my ceiling and the ceiling fan and the steady scream of the AC unit in the window.

I should note the euphoria after it's over. The profound contentment. Practically religious. I can understand confusing that moment for divinity.

Hildie and I take Dolores to dinner at our favorite Mexican restaurant. We've come here so often that the waitstaff greets us with shouts when we arrive. We've bridged the divide between customer and acquaintance. Hildie thought to call ahead to tell them KJ died, so they wouldn't ask about him. Turns out they'd already seen the obituary in the paper. "We all wept," one of our regular servers told her.

I worry coming here will trigger too many memories. I worry that the taste of this salsa will be forever tainted by loss. I wonder if there's any sort of euphoria on the other side of grief.

Hildie sits next to Dolores. I sit next to an empty chair.

We all pluck nachos from the basket. We each have our own ramekin of salsa. The waitstaff long ago learned we consume too much salsa to share.

Dolores is in her usual Dolores clothes, a curated wardrobe of vintage shop finds. Nothing ever fancy, but the arrangement always works. I don't know why I expected different.

She eats a mound of fajita, no leftovers. We talk about the usual topics. Books and art. Hell, there's even laughter.

This could just be a day KJ had to work late. We could be meeting him at a bar after dinner.

We finish eating. Dolores straightens the table, stacking the plates, putting balled-up napkins in the empty nacho basket. We pay and walk north toward the river. As locals this isn't a place we'd usually go, but Dolores suggests it, and she's got a few weeks left of us deferring to all her suggestions.

My stomach is raw. My belches reek of salsa. I keep them quiet, but Hildie hears one and chortles. She finds nothing funnier than bodily functions. She and KJ would have lengthy exchanges using only lip-farts.

River Street is predictably full of tourists. It's early enough that the families are still out but late enough that the drunks are, too, stumbling over cobblestones.

A crowd gathers around a man on a unicycle, juggling. As if one of those activities alone wouldn't do. The unicycle is extra tall. He hovers above the heads of the spectators. The juggling pins traverse mighty arcs through the sky.

The buildings on River Street form a unified front. Aged brick and patches of newer brick marking repairs. Restaurants, bars, and t-shirt shops occupy the ground floors. I have no idea what's behind the higher windows.

There's a sailing ship moored at the dock. Several times a year, some ship or other makes port and charges people ten bucks for a tour. This ship belongs to the Coast Guard. Kids swarm the deck like an infestation.

We walk on. The crowds eddy and swirl. The flow bottlenecks, though it's not clear why. People are tides.

Music from the pavilion carries over the din. Jazz, maybe?

The Savannah River courses brown with sediment and whatever else they dumped in upstream.

Dolores and Hildie hold hands, swinging their arms in an exaggerated motion. I lag a few steps behind. I'm struck by how close abnormality lies to normalcy. They're nearly the same state.

KJ could just be late at work.

There's another juggler, and for a moment I'm not sure if we haven't made a complete loop. But this juggler doesn't ride a unicycle. No cycle of any sort. I wonder if the little girl dropping a dollar bill into his tip jar would be so generous if she knew about the better act up the street.

The little girl toddles directly away from her parents. They wave and call out from the other side of the circle formed around the juggler. She exits the circle and approaches the edge of the riverwalk. There's a single measly chain keeping people in. It's ten, fifteen feet down to the water. The little girl's parents sprint through the open space of the circle, almost knocking the juggler down. I calculate their speed versus the speed of their daughter's toddling. They won't make it in time. The girl's thumb-sized sandals slap the cement. Jeezus, I think. I'm frozen. There's a whole crowd of people and we're all totally stuck watching this shit about to happen.

And then Dolores is there, and she has the girl's arm, this blip of a person barely more than a baby, and then Dolores is carrying the girl and handing her back to the parents.

The slapping noise continues, but it's my pulse.

The parents envelop their daughter. The dad is weeping. The kid is oblivious.

Dolores averts her face.

The juggler's several balls still orbit. Impressive concentration.

"You have to be careful around here," says Dolores.

It's dim in the evening now. You can't tell she's crying unless the streetlights hit her eyes. The parents grovel and profess thanks, and then they're lost among the tourists.

Near-death is as sneaky as death, here and gone before you have a chance to name it.

My headache returns as an explosion. No aura. No warning. A jarring pain in the spot behind my eye. I guess I gasped because Hildie is standing right in front of me.

"Are you OK?" she asks.

"Jeezus," I say. An involuntary reaction has my hand clutching my head.

Dolores comes over, tears gone, mouth agape.

I lower my hand from my head and force my expression to relax. Head pain has to be the stuff of her nightmares. Mine, too. How often have I imagined KJ when the stroke hit? Sometimes I imagine other deaths for him, too, like falling.

"What's happening?" asks Dolores.

"Migraine," I say.

I pat my pockets hoping for a loose ibuprofen, but of course there's nothing like that.

"Since when do you have migraines?"

I don't tell Dolores when they started. It feels important not to.

"I need to go home," I say.

"Can you walk?" asks Hildie.

Can I? Walking seems unlikely. The pain moors me. I can walk only as far as the length of the rope.

"I'll get a ride," I say.

"Do you need anything?" asks Dolores.

"You two enjoy the rest of the night."

I hug them both and head back toward Bay Street. I climb the old stone steps by City Hall. Each step entrenches the hurt deeper in the tissues of my head.

Small miracle, there's an empty cab idling at the stoplight at the top of the steps. I give my address. My consciousness slips below the hurt. I don't remember the ride or paying or getting into bed.

I wake up and the hurt has been replaced with euphoria.

A feeling like almost falling, but someone's there to snatch you back.

March 24
...

It wasn't until the 1920s that word *headache* came to mean "an annoying or bothersome person, situation, activity, etc." But that's a century now of a connotation of slightness. A thing to be brushed aside or ignored. A thing to avoid whenever possible.

A person with a headache that's worse than an annoyance becomes a headache to their friends.

March 25

...

As soon as the phosphenes appear, I take two ibuprofens. And then two more when I doubt the first dose will do the trick. The aura is less pronounced than usual, the hurt muted, a hint at what would happen without the pills.

My tongue is numb and puffy. I'm not sure how puffy it normally is.

In the later stages of the aura, I see fortress walls, built of heavy stones and crenelated along the top. The walls turn ghostly and evaporate.

I'm scared to move. Moving might summon the hurt full force.

I sit in my desk chair by the window. Lying down makes the pain worse and allows it to spread. I periodically browse bed frames with headboards on the Ikea website.

The light outside has that morning quality, extra yellow. Sunrise catches windows.

I've already left a message for my boss. She knows I'll catch up on any missed work. If I have a skill, it's to edit shitty local television commercials faster than anyone else on the planet. The trick is to care more than most editors but not enough to ever slow down.

KJ's drawing is taped to the wall by the window.

"You gonna stay inside all day?" asks the corgi in KJ's voice.

KJ never liked to be at home. Home was for sleep. Being awake meant being out.

"Dude," I say. "I'm not getting up."

I haven't given the corgi a name, but now that it's talking in KJ's voice, I guess it's basically him. At least the corgi isn't competing with a living person for the name.

"Let's do something," says the corgi.

"Sure, why not."

It seems safe to humor a hallucination.

The corgi emerges from the paper and assumes larger-than-corgi proportions. Smaller than an adult human, bigger than a child. The definitive size of a sidekick, though I'm the one following him.

We walk through downtown toward City Market. It was morning when we left, but now it's night. Orange-hued lamps shine through the branches of oak trees in the squares. The muggy breeze is a wet smack on the skin. We pass friends on the sidewalk. I ask where they're going, but nobody replies.

I remain aware of the pain in my head, a new sort of awareness, drawing my attention to parts of my anatomy where I didn't know I had nerve endings. What other parts of myself might I notice given the right stimulation?

The corgi and I descend to Square Bar, situated in a City Market basement. It's an okay space, but we never come here. On weekends, it turns into body spray central. Tonight, or today, or whatever time it is in my head, the bar is quiet. The usual bros and their bro-sweat aren't around to fug up the place. The corgi orders KJ's favorite beer and I have a bourbon. I can't taste it. My tongue is numb.

A table in a side room is set up with one of those giant Jenga-type games made from lengths of two-by-four, where you pull out a block of wood, set it on top, and try not to topple the tower. We go to the table at the corgi's suggestion and begin playing.

The corgi proves adept at grabbing blocks between his thumbless forepaws. I'm less skilled despite my evolutionary advantages.

"It's interesting to think," says the corgi, "that the initial state of the blocks, the neat stack, contains all the potential for chaos. There's energy in the stack. We increase that as we play, moving it closer and closer to tumbling. When the tower finally falls, that's chaos doing its thing."

The corgi places a block on the top of the stack with a clunk. I place the next one. Footsteps on boardwalks. The corgi sips his beer. Somehow, he's able to hold the beer with one paw. The bottle sticks there. Physics is all sorts of fucked up.

We take turns back and forth. The tower grows in both height and precariousness.

"That's weird," I say, "how a thing can be made taller without adding anything new to it."

"What the hell are you talking about?" asks the corgi.

I'm a little miffed since I listened to his spiel about chaos without complaint.

The tower's bottom layers are down to single central blocks. I set my drink on the table. The tower wobbles. It tips, spilling to the filthy concrete floor. Such a racket.

I have to pee.

I look up and I'm back in my apartment and the corgi rests motionless on the paper. When I stand my head throbs, but not hard, not enough to trigger a full-fledged migraine.

The bathroom window has basically the same view as from my chair. It's later, judging by the light, but still morning.

March 26
...

A tall stack of DVCPRO tapes looms on my desk when I get into work. Black bricks with yellow flaps, layered with old labels. Tapes are a bad sign because it means the footage hasn't been digitized. We used to have a production assistant who handled stuff like that, but we haven't hired a replacement since they quit last year.

I carry the tapes to the newsroom, the only place in the building with a functional DVCPRO deck. The newsroom is clusters of desks and florescent lights and people looking busy at computers. The edit stations line the right wall. Sitting at one is like being in detention.

I flip the power on the deck. It wheezes to life. The chassis is held together with gaffer's tape. The scent of hot electrical.

I plop the tape in the slot and shuttle forward to the first frame of video. The video is in standard definition, but the client will absolutely want it to look good in high def.

To clients everywhere I say, this is impossible.

I digitize the video without thought. We used to call the process *capturing*.

The muscles of my hand recognize the feel of the shuttle knob. As a PA, I ran tapes for newscasts, juggling three decks at once. We haven't used tapes for newscasts in forever.

The video turns familiar. Knickknacks, tchotchkes, a thousand novelty cat items. Useless, joy-bringing shit. I haven't found the exterior shot yet, but I remember it, a strip mall gift shop. I made a commercial using this video back when I first started as an editor. The past surges to the present. I can't believe this shop is still in business.

Time and space are bullshit.

Mike Chow comes over and asks how I'm doing. He hung out with me and KJ a few times. Mike Chow's the youngest, most single news anchor. He always talks in announcer-voice, rollercoastering his diction even when he's drunk. We always call him by his full name.

"Been a weird month," I answer.

"Let me know, you know, if you need anything."

"Yeah, man."

I return to my work. The second tape features ceramic Christmas villages. Tiny shops, houses, city halls, and barns, all coated in glittery snow. Lilliputian people milling about. Pea-sized stocking caps and shoelace scarves.

We're nowhere near the holiday season, but I digitize the video anyway. If I don't, the client will absolutely come back in November asking for it. I hum "Good King Wenceslas." The reporter at the next desk glances at me. I hum louder.

I eject the tape. The machine grunts. It needs a minute. Who doesn't? I stretch and twist the spinny chair to face the middle of the room. Working in a noisy building trains you to ignore noises. Now I focus on the keyboard clacks, reporters on phones, crackles of static from the police scanner.

My perspective shifts. I'm a camera looking down at a miniature newsroom. My colleagues are inch high. The basketball on the sports anchor's desk is an orange marble. I reach out, thinking to pluck it up in my fingers. My arm stretches farther than a human arm should. My fingers skew long and alien.

Has the world shrunk or am I growing?

Some of the changes I make to the world during an aura must be permanent.

I turn back to the computer. Perspective looks basically normal in this direction. Except the length of my arm is off. I grab for a tape, but my fingers reach the stack too quickly. The tapes tumble, clattering plastic. So much noise.

The hurt stakes a foothold in my head. It's small and far away. A spark in the distance, approaching. I gather the scattered tapes and hug them to my chest. I go back to my office and chuck the tapes on my desk. The noise is a mistake. I take a couple ibuprofens and sit in the soft lounge chair in the darkest of four dark corners. The chair used to be part of a morning talk show's set.

The world returns to regular size. At least the world inside this room.

Later, I'm back at the computer to finish the edit. I lay down the voiceover, cut by our one ad exec who doesn't have a thick Southern accent. I drop in a sentimental song from the music library. I add Blake's graphics to the end. He's made the giftshop's lavender-colored logo almost readable.

I'm done. The commercial is a blur. I trust that it's fine.

Part of that is I know what I'm doing.

The other part is I know what I do is only ever okay.

March 27

...

The hurt isn't a single thing.

Yes, I can point to a spot on my face beneath which lies the hurt's hypocenter. The spot where the tip of the awl enters my flesh. But the hurt has tendrils. It shifts and cascades. And the existence of the hurt itself makes it hard to localize. Above all else, the hurt wishes to remain unknown.

In one moment, it's white hot behind my eye.

In another it sends witch fingers down my neck.

Sometimes the hurt is a child on a drum set.

Or my scalp will prickle with every sensation except pain, but this absence of pain is also a type of pain.

Sometimes it balloons on my eye from inside my head, trying to pop it out, but instead come tears.

The tears feel too hot.

Other times the need to gasp is the hurt's only sign.

The hurt is a slime that coats me.

The hurt is my insides dissolving into slime.

The hurt bloats the artery on my forehead and turns it tender to the touch.

It hovers in my teeth like rot.

It bunches my eyebrows together, creasing deep wrinkles.

It ages me. I'm getting older, faster per second than the number of seconds.

The number of seconds is infinite.

The hurt is premature. I'm too young to feel this way.

Death is late. This hurt is a harbinger.

Curiously, the hurt isn't sadness. The two can't exist with the same force at the same time.

But sadness isn't the same as depression.

March 28
...

Wittgenstein says pain "is not a something, but not a nothing either!"

Punch the clever bastard's nose and see what he says then.

April 1
...

Coffee shop. Morning. I take my regular spot at the counter between Dolores and Hildie. Usually on April Fool's Day, we'd pull some small prank on each other. Nothing major. Nothing mean. KJ hated meanness.

There are no pranks today. I think Dolores, Hildie, and I all have the same impossible expectation that KJ went big this year, that he'll walk in any minute and sit down on the vacant stool and say *gotcha*. And we'll be like *oh you sonofabitch*. And then next year we'll laugh about it and for years after.

How many more years were there supposed to have been?

Dolores and I are writing as usual—or pretending to. We make a good show of it, at least. Hildie's on her laptop, writing for once, too. She has a solo exhibit coming up at a local gallery and is drafting her artist's statement. She huffs and cusses and hits a bunch of keys with her fist. Strings of random characters stream across her laptop's screen.

"Trouble?" I ask.

"I know what I'm doing when I paint," she says, "and I can talk about it till I puke, but the second I try to put it on paper, it won't come out right."

"Have you tried..." I hold up my hands and wiggle my fingers. "Sorry, writing's magical and can't be explained."

Dolores says, "Maybe tell us about it?"

"Yeah, yeah." Hildie shoves her laptop away. "Basically, I'm looking to art history for depictions of religious miracles and reimagining those paintings through contemporary knowledge. How the unexplained miracles of the past become natural, frankly bland phenomena in the present. Miracles used to happen all the time. But now that we live in an age when everyone has a camera with them twenty-four hours a day, nobody's reporting miracles, much less documenting them. I'm not talking about bullshit like the Blessed Virgin appearing in the sprinkles on a Pop-Tart. All the big religions are built on massive, world-altering miracles that can't be explained by chance. Except, yeah, they can. What's more likely, a deity wrecking Jericho, or a perfectly ordinary earthquake explained after the fact as an act of a god?"

Dolores types while Hildie talks.

"Don't even get me started on visions," continues Hildie. "Every weird-ass thing every prophet ever saw is pretty clearly explicable by what we recognize now as a neurological condition. Take Ezekiel. His visions are consistent with migraine aura. So, I'm remaking Raphael's painting of Ezekiel's vision from the perspective of someone with migraines. There's a lot of migraine art out there as reference. And thanks to you," Hildie reaches up and caresses my temple, "I've refined that idea pretty well."

Dolores pauses typing. "Why's the project important to you?"

"I guess I'm trying to show that the ancient concept of divine beauty has actually created an artificial barrier between the subject of beauty and the perceiver. I'm trying to remove the intermediary. We're all capable of being direct conduits to natural beauty. We don't need magic or miracle for beauty to occur. It's occurring all around us.

"And, finally, I'm just tired of people holding their religious beliefs to be infallible when they're based on an understanding of the world that's outdated by thousands of years. Holding stuff sacred makes us stupid."

"That all sounds fine to me," I say.

"But I can't *write* it."

Dolores taps out a few further words and slides her laptop to Hildie.

"Here," she says.

Hildie reads, nodding, then nodding more emphatically.

"Yes," she says. "Yes!"

People at the next table look up at her shout.

Hildie talks past me to Dolores. "How do you do this?"

Dolores shrugs. "Just things you said."

"But the things I say never make sense."

"This is truth," I say.

Hildie shoves her shoulder into me but holds onto my arm at the same time.

"Where'd you find that stuff on migraines?" I ask.

"This amazing website called Google. I'll send you links."

I give her a thumbs up. Chris stops by with refills. I've already had too much coffee, but I sip out of habit.

The spot in my head where the migraines are worst is raw. Not pain, exactly. Not discomfort. It feels like potential, my body stacking up the pieces of a migraine so they can come tumbling down at any moment.

I take some solace in the idea that I might have this in common with saints.

It's almost nine. Like all good creatives, Hildie and I have to head to day jobs. Dolores is a full-time writer and freelances from home, but she usually leaves the coffee shop when we do. I slip cash under my half-empty coffee cup. Gallery is the last establishment in the universe that doesn't accept cards. Hildie is a dollar short so I loan her the difference. One of us always forgets to bring enough cash. Dolores arranges our abandoned stools in a perfect line.

Outside, Hildie heads north toward Telfair, the art museum where she works as a preparator. Dolores and I head south together. There's an early bloom of star jasmine intertwining a wrought iron fence. The flowers blanket the sidewalk in sickly sweet. The pain in my head flares but drops away immediately.

I dare a look at Dolores. I try to read how she's feeling in her expression. There's no clue to be found.

We were the first two members of Breakfast Club. We met in a writing group and started writing together in the mornings. I remember that year when it was just the two of us. If the group had never grown, we wouldn't be where we are now. We'd never have gained what we've lost.

We pass the apartment where my ex-girlfriend Jill used to live. This small city is full of memories.

A car comes from behind us. Drayton Street is one way in the opposite direction. Out-of-town plates. I wave at the driver to warn them, but they're clueless. Another car turns onto Drayton from a side street, heading the right way. The tourist slams the brakes. No crash. Lots of honking horns.

"Sometimes I imagine him in accidents." Dolores has stopped walking. "That's easier to understand than what happened."

"I have nightmares like that," I say.

I have an imagining as clear as memory of KJ falling off a cliff.

The traffic situation fixes itself. The horns go quiet. I think of a tangled string freeing its own knots. We start walking again.

A kid from the art college rolls by on a skateboard. Another on a bike, no helmet. So much precarious shit, everywhere you look.

Dolores and I hug and part ways at the next intersection.

Back then, it was just the two of us, and honestly, I can't decide whether or not it would have been better if that's how it stayed.

The risks versus the rewards of loving more people.

The more friends you collect, the more likely it is that one of them falls.

My Personal History of Pain
Part II
...

I noticed her stack of books before I saw her. This was about five years ago. The woman had come into the coffee shop and taken one of the comfy chairs. From her generic Jansport backpack, she produced one book after another, paperback editions of the classics. A surprising number of Russians. That first day, she pulled the top book off the stack, *Moby Dick*, judging from the breaching whale on the cover. She was there reading when Breakfast Club adjourned for the day, and she was there again the next morning when I arrived. Two days later, she was done with *Moby Dick* and deep into Dostoevsky.

This went on for a month. The book stack growing shorter, a book finished every couple days, sometimes replenished with new titles, but the overall impression was one of unstacking. Time progressing, hourglass sand.

One weeknight I met KJ at the coffee shop after work. Sometimes our restlessnesses aligned, and we'd both want nothing more than to be anywhere other than home. KJ was like that always, I guess, so maybe I should say for once my restlessness aligned with his. We took a table by the window. It must have been spring. I should know the exact date. The kid who played violin in the square was out, his music a faint whine through the glass. It'd been fun over the years to hear him get better and better and better.

KJ tapped my hand on the table with the backs of his fingers. "The Woman with the Books," he said.

That's what we called her.

She entered and, finding her preferred spot occupied, took one of the sofas. We knew to never sit there because the wall-mounted AC unit blew directly in your face if you did. Even on the hottest Savannah day, that spot was intolerably cold.

The woman set out her books and stacked them, eyed the AC unit, and removed a cardigan from her bag, too. I watched her, because I guess my crush by this point was surging full-force, the kind you can only have for a nameless other, when you can project all you want and hope and dream onto them.

"When are you going to talk to her?" asked KJ.

"Because that's exactly what a woman reading alone at a coffee shop wants, to have some dude interrupt her?"

"You read at home if you want solitude."

"What do you know about either home or solitude?"

"For solitude, I've got you as reference. When was your last date?"

The numbers were too large, the math too complex, to answer quickly.

"You don't even know, bro," said KJ.

"I'm not going to interrupt her reading," I said.

"Have it your way. Your lonely, destined-to-die-alone way."

I toasted him with my empty mug. "Here's to a long, pathetic life."

After that, I made myself not look in her direction. The orange lights were on in the square, casting up on the undersides of oak leaves. The violinist was gone. I hadn't noticed the music stop. A group of tourists followed a guide dressed as a colonist. Other tourists pulled low-hanging moss from the trees and draped themselves with it like shawls. The moss is full of redbugs, basically mite-sized ticks. Locals know better than to touch it. So many tourists.

"If I ever write about Savannah," I said, "I'm never going to describe the Spanish moss."

"Folks love the fucking moss, though," said KJ. "Give the people what they want."

At some point, I had to pee, so I got up, which took me on a wending path among the clusters of furniture, bunches of little living rooms, and near the couch where the Woman with the

Books had moved on to a new paperback, Toni Morrison, I thought, recognizing the particular hue of maroon on the cover. I tried to twist back to confirm my guess without being obvious.

That's when I whacked my shin into the coffee table.

I can't describe that specific instance of pain, but I've been clumsy often enough that I can offer its likeliest progression. The shock of the initial impact turned quickly hot, and then shot up and down the whole shin bone, and then coursed into the surrounding muscle, and then sank deeper into core tissues, and then into spaces that weren't even part of my body, as if pain could tunnel backward to earlier bodies, as if pain was always, always there, part of what holds the nuclei of atoms together, and here my clumsy ass was fissioning the very glue of the universe. And all I could do in the face of this cosmic destruction was to hiss inward through my teeth and futilely rub the site of my future bruise.

"Are you alright?" asked the Woman with the Books.

She set the Morrison back on the stack and looked into my eyes. And here's the thing: that pain—which had consumed every part of me and still hurt just as much as it had a moment ago—faded so far into the background that it might as well have belonged to somebody else. How much better off might we all be if every doctor's visit was replaced by a meet-cute?

"Just awkward is all," I said. "*Beloved?*" I asked, pointing to the cover of the Morrison I could now clearly see.

"Going through all her works," said the Woman with the Books. "A glaring hole in my personal library. I'm Jill."

I introduced myself.

"So, you're a reader?" she asked.

"A writer," I said.

"That's what you're doing here every morning?"

Heat swelled in my cheeks that she'd noticed me.

"At least what I try to do. Can't promise I always end up writing something."

She invited me to sit, so I did, ignoring my full bladder. We talked about books and writing and then about other things, but like pain, there's a blur here, too, this memory combined with our first few dates, the whole getting-to-know-you phase overlapping.

KJ stood from the table where I'd abandoned him. He was all grinning imp as he waved goodbye. He wasn't living with Dolores yet, but I knew he'd call her as soon as he got outside. He'd tell her everything that happened. I knew the next morning at Breakfast Club I'd be bashful.

"Didn't mean to steal you from your friend," Jill said.

"Borrowed," I replied. "It's fine."

And it was. Sore shin, burning bladder, every tiny discomfort soothed away, warm and numb and contented.

Here was the panacea I've been looking for ever since the day Jill moved away, the day I chose not to follow. When I was young and thought all wounds healed, given time.

April 5

The CVS sells ibuprofen in extra-large bottles. Hundreds of pills. Think milk jug. Like I'm planning to dump that shit in my coffee every morning and have at it.

Maybe I will. All I aim for is numbness.

I also buy a pill fob, an aluminum tube with a screw-on cap, pocket-sized. If I medicate immediately after the aura starts, the migraine doesn't get as bad. I'm an ibuprofen quickdraw. The Wild West of pain relief.

I pack the fob full and head out. I have a lunch date today. A second date. I went out once with Kat back before KJ died, and then sort of forgot about her, all things considered, and now I figure I should go out again.

The wind musses my hair, but it's usually messed up anyway.

I stop by the coffee shop because I skipped Breakfast Club and need caffeine. I wave to Chris. The coffeemaker spurts out the last drips of a fresh carafe. Chris brings a cup over.

Outside, the ancient oak trees in the square go berserk. Spanish moss blows perpendicular. Dead leaves cartwheel over the sidewalk. Jetsam pings the windows.

The caffeine mixes with my blood. I'm so much more aware now of the processes within my body.

I sense the hurt is coming before it begins.

I take two ibuprofens with my coffee. I could take another—there are a thousand of the damn pills back at my apartment—but I'm pacing myself. A fear of diminishing returns.

The hurt doesn't care about the ibuprofen. It's pounding hard to the front of my consciousness. There's no aura. I've come to rely on the aura as an early warning system.

I'm supposed to meet Kat in fifteen minutes.

I hang on for a few minutes more.

I call Kat. I have a migraine, I tell her. Her voice sounds distant, which is for the best because she's super pissed.

"First, no contact in weeks, and then you set something up and cancel it at the last second. Fuck you. Get your act together."

This is unexpected. Being sick, you expect sympathy. On the heels of grief, you expect understanding.

"Yeah," I say, "okay," and hang up.

At least I won't have to worry about a third date.

Later, in the pain's waning, I'm sitting at my desk, alternating between staring out my window and staring at shit on the internet.

Six stories below, I can see the back door to the karaoke bar on the corner. Whenever someone comes or goes, tortured singing escapes. My windows are old and thin and single paned.

KJ always felt like singing at the end of a night out. He always picked a song by Bowie. He wasn't half-bad.

One time, I got roofied in the karaoke bar. I recall the sensation of being drugged, the tunnel vision, the shadows creeping in from behind. I feel like that now.

The inside of my mouth is inflamed. My nose, too. If I'm honest, also my asshole. Any inside part of me that connects to the outside world has a mild burn. This is a new and disconcerting symptom.

In the aftermath of the hurt, I obsess over it. Pain is supposed to be a message from the body to the mind, isn't it? But it's more basic than that. I think about pain in terms of physics. The way I feel at any moment is part of a massive machine, the universe, transferring energy from one state to another. When I hurt, all that's happening is the most efficient method of moving energy. In that way, pain fulfills a function. The same function as everything else.

Stars are pain machines and black holes are pain machines and slugs oozing slime trails across old rotten logs are pain machines.

Pain was coded into the information of the universe at the Big Bang. All pain was once contained in an infinitesimal point.

Before the beginning, before stuff spread out, the universe hurt completely.

Wanting pain to have a special meaning is human arrogance. Pain is the opposite of meaning, a reminder that nothing means shit. That makes me feel less bad about bailing on Kat.

Below, an early-drunk couple stumbles into the karaoke bar. Inside, some asshole is singing "Piano Man." He'll keep singing it until the end of time.

When the last flicker of pain fades out, that's the end. That's the death of the universe. This is a self-serving thought, that only my pain perpetuates existence. Or maybe it's a wish.

Would I trade everything for nothing? Day by day, that deal seems fairer.

The door to the bar closes. No more music, at least not that I can hear.

April 6

Anne Boyer writes of her cancer and recovery: "In pain, the spatial becomes temporal, as in *pain is the experience of a location that exists only as desperation for its end.*"

Time and space are bullshit.

April 7

I wake up scared. My head threatens. At any moment it might tip over into migraine. When the sunlight flashes through the branches of a live oak, I fear it's the start of an aura. A small pain always inhabits the spot where the hurt will come.

I get a coffee but don't stay for Breakfast Club. I'm taxed by the thought of being social.

Back at my desk with the corgi drawing. I'm scared, too, of motion. I fear every unknown trigger.

Who's aiming the gun and who will fire it?

The corgi talks to me in KJ's voice.

"You gonna stay in here forever?" he asks.

I hold my head as if that's the same as reaching inside and holding the part that aches.

The corgi climbs out of the picture and resumes his larger size. Streaks mar his highlighter fur, the edges of his Sharpie outline rough.

The corgi goes into the hall closet and comes out wearing my raincoat. It shouldn't fit, but it does. Out the window the sun is shining. No clouds.

"Come on," says the corgi.

We're on the sidewalk, striding in the direction of the river. We keep not turning. This is a surprise because KJ wouldn't visit River Street on a bet. His tourist tolerance is impossibly low.

We descend the steps to River Street and go to the Coast Guard cutter moored at the dock. We board via the gangplank and join the families pointing at ropes and asking questions. The corgi tenses. Even this version of KJ dislikes tourists.

He draws a cutlass from within the raincoat. He chases all the parents over the gunwales and into the water, but he lets the kids stick around. *Shove off*, he calls, and the kids obey. I'm impressed with their efficiency. I'm impressed they know which ropes work what.

The ship drifts from the dock. The sails unfurl and bulge in the wind. The kids, our crew, go astern and wave to their parents, dogpaddling in the water. The parents wave back.

We leave River Street behind and pass into the channel. Tybee Island slides by. We sail a thousand miles into the ocean. I can tell we're far away from home because there are no more seagulls.

The waves rise in massive swells. The ship is a bug. We crawl up one side of the water and slip down the other. A pod of whales swims beneath us. The children squee with delight. The sun on the water reflects every star shooting by at once. The constellations shift, which makes them not constellations.

Normally, I get motion sickness in an instant. Whatever this trip is, though, it's not motion. I feel the rise and fall, but also I don't. Maybe I only think the motion.

"Of course you only think it," says the corgi.

We crest a swell and I spot a disturbance in the distance. I confirm it at the top of the next swell. We're approaching a great dome in the water. It towers over the other waves. On each sighting it's grown more. It's a monument or a skyscraper or a mountain.

"Up ahead," I shout.

The corgi climbs to the crow's nest. I follow him up.

"We need to turn," I say.

"Nonsense," says the corgi. "*This* is what we came for."

The kid at the wheel aims us straight for the wall of water. A quiver of friction passes through the hull and up the mast and into my feet.

"What is it?" I ask.

"A rogue wave!" declares the corgi. "In a system like the ocean, sometimes conditions turn out right for all the pent-up energy to focus on a single point."

The rogue wave sucks up lesser waves like it's slurping soup. If our ship was a bug before, then now it's a mote.

"That's one thing people don't understand," says the corgi. "The universe tends to create little pockets of order. A planet is like a rogue wave, a place where all the churning forces of creation happen to coalesce. A person is the same. Or a corgi!"

We're so close to the rogue wave now, there's no escaping it. The bow pitches up. The boat is nearly vertical. I'm pinned against the back of the crow's nest. The kids fall off the deck and into the ocean. Our pilot clings to the wheel, but a fist of water pelts her. When the spray and foam clear, she's gone.

We're halfway up the wave. The wood of the ship emits sharp cries. Timbers crack deep within the structure. The corgi dons a pirate hat.

The column of water finally breaks and crashes over us. There's so much water we're completely inside it, drowned. I cleave to the crow's nest. Sharp currents try to tear me away. A fish slaps into my face. More streak by. Silver bolts. The sails rip from the masts and flow prettily in the water. They move slower than everything else, elegant dancers amid a riot. Then the sails are far behind us and disappear.

How long can I hold my breath?

We break the surface. I think of standing atop a gray cloud, watching a storm from above. The battered ship levels out. We're on smooth seas. The rogue wave thunders away. It shrinks smaller and smaller until it's a regular wave and then nothing. My skin pricks with the euphoria of survival.

The corgi lost his hat along the way.

"So, yeah," says the corgi. "Chaos."

I'm back at my desk and the corgi is confined again to paper.

Moisture slicks my skin. Sweat, not seawater.

"Find it," says the corgi.

But, like usual, he offers no more guidance than that.

April 14
...

The coffee shop has a different crowd at night. Loners. The dispossessed. People who can tolerate espresso after 7pm. Toward the end of each semester, the shop floods with art school kids writing papers or picking up huge to-go cups to take back to studios.

Then there are the people still wearing work clothes. Wrinkled, untucked, frumpier than when they set out in the morning. Why the delay getting home? What monsters await there? Family or the lack thereof. Endless sitcoms.

I sit on one of the couches. I try not to think about the billion drinks that have been spilled on it. I avoid touching surfaces like I'm back in the doctor's office. All furniture in a coffee shop ends up browner than not.

It must be Wednesday because Preacherman is here. He's a doughy, middle-aged nobody, but somehow he's managed to curate a small flock of followers. The followers are young, art school kids, possibly high schoolers. Preacherman puts forth a jovial front. Cheeks like Santa. Loose blond curls nest atop his head.

Dolores comes in and almost flips right around. She *hates* Preacherman. She can't tune him out. She seethes at every dumbass word he utters. Such words abound. I expect one day for her to grab him by his stupid curls and shake him.

I don't know if she hates the content of what he says or his smugness. I've always found him a blowhard but harmless.

Dolores joins me on the dank couch. She slumps into the cushions. She's in her work clothes, but she works from home, so maybe she's not.

"Anything interesting today?" I ask.

"New album to review, but I can't concentrate. I'll put the album on and it'll be over and I remember none of it."

Most of Dolores's freelance work is music reviews. She knows more bands than anybody, from rap to jazz to K-pop. One whole wall of her apartment is shelves filled with LPs.

Preacherman is loud-talking about Jesus walking on water and attempting to connect that to turning water into wine. His theology goes only as deep as recognizing the same word in different places in the Bible.

"Have you been sleeping?" I ask.

Preacherman references a recent movie with a boat in it.

"I've been thinking about getting a new bed," says Dolores.

"Water is a liquid," says Preacherman, pausing to let the profundity of that sink in.

Dolores bolts upright. "For chrissake," she says, too loud. She falls back into the cushions and scowls.

She flicks her hand at a half-eaten scone on a saucer left on the table.

"Scones are a solid," she says, quieter. "And you're a bloated bag of gas."

I cover my mouth to stifle a laugh. Laughing hurts my head, or it's trying not to laugh that does it. Pain pings behind my eye. It pings louder and louder, an enemy submarine closing in. I force myself to relax. I push away the levity. The hurt recedes to the background. Not leaving, waiting.

KJ was the best at riffing off Preacherman's bullshit. He used to plan to be here on Wednesday evenings to eavesdrop. To crack jokes at this Gomer's expense. The dumber the thing Preacherman said, the happier it made KJ.

KJ would have loved "Water is a liquid." I hear his delighted cackle in my head.

Years ago, I wrote down this quote from KJ in my notebook: Let people believe what they want, but that guy? He wants a cult, but he's not charismatic enough to get one, so he dupes a bunch of kids with quasi-biblical platitudes and tries to pass off 'don't have sex until marriage' as divine goddamn wisdom.

It's true. I've overheard Preacherman's coffee shop sermons for a decade. He's never approached profundity. He relies on the ignorance of the kids. He relies on their conflicted horniness. And I don't mean that these kids are especially ignorant, just that they're kids. They're vulnerable. Susceptible. There's a reason his little flock constantly cycles through new members. Even an ignorant kid eventually picks up on the bullshit.

Preacherman drinks red wine, a single glass each Wednesday. Like it's a sacrament. Like it makes him look cool. None of his followers are old enough to join him.

Nobody reacted to his water wisdom, so now he talks louder, riling himself up.

"You gotta get this right, and right now" he says. He points downward to the exact location of the present moment. His Southern accent thickens. "If you don't get this right and you died tomorrow, you'd go to Hell. The people in this room, they're all going to Hell. Everyone you pass on the street, they're going to Hell, too. And that's where they deserve to be, but you're different. You're saved."

Dolores pantomimes gagging on her own finger.

"I can't handle this," she says.

She hugs me sideways and grabs all the random cups and saucers from the table to return to the counter. She waves as she leaves. I'd walk with her, but the threat of pain has me moored.

Outside, a horse clops by pulling a carriage filled with tourists.

Preacherman's meeting ends. The kids disperse. He returns his wine glass to the counter and acts super nice to Chris, which I guess is a point in Preacherman's favor.

He stops by the low mantle over the gas fireplace. A faint whiff of spoiled eggs lingers there from the pilot light. The mantle is littered with flyers for events and art exhibitions and local businesses. People drop off that stuff all the time, but hardly anybody looks at it. Some of the flyers are for events that happened years ago.

Preacherman lifts a postcard and outright scowls. With an audience, he's all smiles and sincerity. His cheeks flush with wine. Now, he's pale and vile. Now he's devilish. A creature of the hot passions he cautions against.

My first thought: what a fucking hypocrite. And then: how terrifying.

He rips the postcard down the middle and drops the halves back on the mantle. He composes his face before he turns to leave.

That's a sermon I can appreciate: Don't force others to endure what's inside you.

Before I go, I check the mantle. I hold the two halves of the postcard together. It's one of Hildie's paintings for her upcoming show. The back features the artist's statement that Dolores wrote. The exhibit is still months away. I didn't know Hildie had made flyers.

I've seen the painting on the flyer before, at least in progress. It's Hildie's interpretation of Raphael's "Saint George and the Dragon." Her Saint George is in a Western-themed bar, riding a mechanical bull, spilling beer from a bottle. The beer splashes on the floor into the shape of a dragon. A clichéd cowgirl watches it all from the background.

I take the ripped card home. I tape it back together. I tack it next to KJ's drawing of the corgi on the wall.

April 15
...

Patrick Wall, a pioneer of pain research, muses, "the entire subject of pain encompasses one of the last taboos."

We present stiff upper lips. We accept *suffering* as *Christ-like*. We get what we deserve.

But that's all bullshit nobility. That's an argument for pain to have a meaning, a purpose, a hope on the other side. Whole religions are built on that kind of thinking.

Because it's easier to look away from pain than toward it.

April 16

Elaine Scarry notes that pain "takes no object," that *I hurt* is intransitive. But there's a palindromic implication, like the unspoken *you* in a command: *I hurt I*. If the body is mine, then the pain inflicted on the body is inflicted by me.

It's not the stab of the knife that hurts, but the body deciding the wound is a problem.

April 18
...

Blake texts me that I should probably hoof it over to Pinkie's. The bar is around the corner from my apartment. The sun is still up. I pull on pants and slip on sneakers and get there in five.

Dolores is at the two-seater booth near the bathrooms. Her butt's in the seat, but her upper half sprawls across the table. Her breaths are tiny animals.

I order a water and a bourbon from Matt at the bar. I claim the other side of the booth and give Dolores the water. Her head is sideways, cheek smooshed flat. She taps her fingers on the tabletop and watches the water ripple. Her eyes are swimmy.

"Hey, Doll," I say.

"Hey, motherfucker." She laughs, a sound akin to drowning.

This here is role reversal. Dolores never gets sloppy drunk. She looks out for the rest of us. She's gifted with both tolerance and responsibility.

Her body twists. She's forming herself into a Möbius loop. Her movements happen in a different timeline than the one I'm in. It makes me think of scrolling through videos at work, jerks then lulls then whole minutes skipped. Time and space are bullshit.

Blake wanders over and we tap plastic cups. He squeezes Dolores's shoulder, but she doesn't react.

"How's your head been?" Blake asks me.

"It keeps reminding me it's there," I say.

He points to my cup. "Is the whiskey a good idea?"

"Only idea I got."

Blake goes back to the bar and sits next to some guy I don't know. The guy has a bit of a pompadour, but he pulls it off. He's drinking red wine, which, in Pinkie's standard plastic cup, looks like juice.

"So, what's up?" I ask Dolores. "Blake said there was trouble."

Dolores gathers herself into a seated position. I suspect she's not as drunk as she's acting.

"I punched a dude in the ear," she says.

"Anyone we know?"

"Just a dude. He was hitting on me."

I scan the bar for a bleeding ear.

"He's gone." she says. "Matt kicked him out."

"Drink some water," I say.

She lifts the cup and takes bird sips.

"My mom left today," she says.

Dolores's mom had stayed in town since KJ's memorial. Cooking and cleaning and all that. Making sure her daughter didn't collapse into herself. As if one can be shielded from hurt that's already happened. Her mom lives far away in Texas.

"Can you walk?" I ask.

"I've got legs, motherfucker."

That Dolores can joke seems a positive sign. I leave cash on Jimmy Carter's plaque on the bar as we exit. I wave to Blake, but he's getting handsy with the unknown guy and doesn't see me. Dolores grabs a stray napkin someone left on a table and tosses it in the garbage can by the door.

The sun has yet to set. I keep forgetting it's no longer winter. Yellow pollen stains the sidewalk. It smells like rain is on the way. There's a short thunderstorm most evenings in spring. The storms sweep in, downpour, flash and bang, and then flee to the ocean. The clouds haven't arrived, though, so there's time.

Traffic grumbles by on Drayton, so I lead us to a side street. We pass into Lafayette Square by the cathedral. The sun hits the front of the twin spires.

Our pace is as slow as possible but still considered movement.

"You just felt like hitting the dude?" I ask.

"I felt like hitting. The dude happened to be there."

Dolores makes the sign of the cross. She's very much not Catholic.

"Praying?" I ask.

"Fuck that noise." She raises two middle fingers, one for each cross atop each spire. She drops her hands, dead weights. "The dude wasn't that bad. I mean, yeah, he saw a drunk woman at a bar and thought he had a shot. But he wasn't gross about it. He would have walked away without a fuss if I'd asked. That's not why I hit him."

We take a turtle-paced lap of the fountain in the square's center. The sound of the water ripples the air.

"There's this constant ache," she says. "Right in the middle of me, like I took a cannon to the stomach. There's a hole there and it's filled with phantom pains. I wanted someone else to have that feeling. It doesn't feel fair that I have to feel it alone."

"You can punch me whenever you want," I say.

She gives me her *shut up, dumbass* look. I've received it often.

We leave Lafayette Square and cross two more streets and enter Troup Square. The Unitarian church here, finished in pinkish stone, always reminds me of a fairytale palace.

The sun is lower. This part of town offers a hush.

"It's a desperate feeling," she says. "I've never felt this intensely before."

"I think it's only possible to feel this way a few times in life. At least I hope that's the case."

The bros are in the square behind us before I notice. Three of them. Any of them bigger than me. One leads, the other two a step behind. The lead bro strides up to Dolores.

"Look what you did, goddammit." He points to his ear. The lobe is a cocktail cherry.

"Wow, have you been working out?" I say. "Gettin' swole."

One of the bro's friends laughs. The lead bro turns super pissed. He bumps his chest into me.

"Listen, bro," I say. "We're not having the best of days."

"Damn right, you're not."

He punches the side of my head. I guess he was aiming for the ear, some Hammurabi bullshit, but missed. There wasn't a lot of force behind the hit, but I take a knee from the shock of it. I yelp. Kind of an embarrassing sound.

A light flips on in the upstairs window of the closest townhome. A man's silver-haired head pokes out.

"I'm calling the cops!" the man shouts down at us.

"Whatever, codger," Dolores shouts back.

The bro's friends laugh.

"Feel better?" I ask the bro.

"You're not gonna fight back?"

Don't get me wrong. I want to pick up a loose brick from the walkway and bash this dude's brain to mush. I want to stomp on his chest till long after his lungs have stopped pumping. I want to spit on his mutilated corpse so the cops will have the DNA evidence they need to prove it was me.

"No," I say.

Dolores helps me up, and we walk away.

"I called the cops." The man waves his glowing cell phone out the window. The townhome must be worth well over a million. That must be his Mercedes parked out front. I hope he drops the phone.

"The cops are on the way," he yells.

Dolores raises both hands and flips him off. Once we exit the square, I glance back, but the bros aren't following.

"You alright?" asks Dolores.

I could say yes, but the jarring to my head has triggered the hurt. Maybe I should have punched back. Maybe I could have transferred some of this pain to the bro. Maybe I could have forced him to share the burden with me. But I wouldn't wish that on anybody.

"I'm fine," I say.

The phosphenes come, falling stars. I'm glad the sun has set. I can see the phosphenes' shine more clearly.

April 23

I go to the doctor today. There have been more migraines, and even when they don't come, it feels as if one will. I've lost whole days waiting. I finished re-watching all seven hundred episodes of *Naruto*. My muscles have softened to sponges from disuse.

I sit in the lobby as far away from coughing people as possible, but everybody's coughing, including the friendly receptionist. The *National Geographic* on the table intrigues me, but not enough to touch its diseased surface. I stare at the cover photo of a glacier. It's broken free from the arctic and begun an impossible journey. I wonder where it's going and if it'll melt before it gets there.

An older guy, prime dad material, descends on the seat next to me. He clears his throat. One cough, and I'll move.

He points to the glacier. "Mind if I take that?"

As if it's my magazine I brought with me and happened to set down on this grimy table.

"Please," I say, "go ahead,"

He thumbs through the magazine. He licks his thumb between pages.

"Global warming, huh?" he says.

"Right?" I say.

I lean back to look at the pictures. Melting glacier after melting glacier. A map shows how much the world's ice has shrunk, how much shrinking is yet to come.

The man slaps the magazine shut as if to say *enough of this global warming bullshit*. He puts the magazine back on the table, face down. The glacier is gone. Global warming, indeed.

"What're you in for?" asks the man.

"Murder," I say.

He chuckles. "These places will drive you to that." He assesses me. "The older you get, the more often you'll visit."

I nod because what do you say to that?

"I had cancer," says the man, "but it's in remission now. *Remission* is the doc's word for needing monthly bloodwork"

"Sorry about that," I say.

"Better than having cancer."

I ponder the profundity of that. It's a philosophy that can only have meaning for someone who's made it to the other side of illness. I try to remember what causes cancer. Bad genes or bad cells or bad blood. Cancer is a betrayal by one's own body.

The nurse cracks open the door and calls my name.

"Happy bloodwork," I say to the man and leave the lobby.

I'm back sitting on the paper-covered examination table. The room is frigid. This can't be conducive to good health. Maybe it prevents germs from multiplying on the room's surfaces. I work with that hypothesis for a while.

The nurse checks my vitals. I've lost a little weight, which I didn't have much of to lose. The nurse says the doctor will be in shortly. The doctor's version of *shortly* and mine don't align.

I shift my butt back and forth to make the paper crinkle.

Whenever I visit the doctor, I'm an imposter. I can't be sufficiently sick to justify taking up her time. Especially today, with no particular pain. What am I doing here? Every doctor's visit is an existential crisis.

The doctor comes in and introduces herself. I was here less than a month ago. She squirts antibacterial goop onto her hands and rubs it in. I notice how dry her hands are, how notably older they look than the rest of her.

She reads one page of my chart, turns to the next page, and then flips back to the first.

"How are the migraines?" she asks.

"They kinda suck," I say.

She smiles. I keep amusing people today.

"How often are they coming on?"

"Two or three times a week," I say. "And one always feels ready to pop up."

She jots a note on the chart. "And are you still treating them with ibuprofen?"

"Yeah. If I take it immediately, it can help stop the pain from escalating."

She nods and jots.

"Have you been keeping a migraine diary?"

"Of a sort."

"Have you noticed any patterns to your headaches? Any activities that might be triggering them?"

"It seems like every activity might be triggering them."

She nods and jots. She sets the chart on the counter.

"I guess the news is both good and bad. You've found a treatment that's helping you cope with migraines. Because of that, and because you're having fewer than fifteen a month, my recommendation is to continue using ibuprofen at the first sign of migraine or as soon as possible after that. However, you need to make sure you don't take too much. If you start taking it daily, it can actually have the opposite effect."

"Got it," I say. "Take ibuprofen, but not too much."

"And keep up with the diary. You never know when a pattern might emerge. We don't know exactly what's happening with migraines, but there are patterns. Knowing those can help us treat them. Anything else?"

"I guess not."

I can't believe I'm about to pay a doctor to tell me *keep on truckin'*.

The doctor leaves and later the nurse directs me back to the front desk. I make a wrong turn. The office is a maze of similar rooms and fluorescent lights. Lost patients wander the halls for years.

I find myself by an emergency exit. There's a coat rack in the corner, so I guess the exit isn't only for emergencies. I snatch a white doctor coat from the rack and drape it over my arm. I check out. The receptionist doesn't mention the coat. I guess that means it's mine.

Outside, I stand in the sun. My office is directly across the street. The broadcast tower is a backlit lattice. I could go in and finish a couple edits this afternoon, but I already took sick leave. I turn around and head to Forsyth Park. I text Dolores to meet me by the fountain.

Steady pedestrian traffic streams through the wide walkway bisecting the length of the park. Mostly tourists. They circle the fountain like a roundabout. Pausing for photos, posing in front of the statues of water-spitting geese.

I select a spot of shade and put on the white coat. I angle myself into the breeze so the coat flutters around me.

Dolores comes up from behind and says, "Doctor?"

That's as far as she'll acknowledge the coat. A person living with KJ had to tolerate mischief.

It's significantly springtime today. Too hot for the coat. We walk south past the cafe and the playground. In the open fields art school kids play a pick-up game of Ultimate.

Dolores asks what the doctor had to say.

"She told me that my headaches aren't bad enough for additional treatment."

"They seem pretty bad to me," says Dolores.

"I'm not arguing with you."

"But the doctor isn't worried?"

She evens her voice, but I see the concern on her face.

"This is a textbook case," I say.

"There's a book?"

Two of the Frisbee kids run into each other full steam. Their bodies produce an audible thump. They get up and dust off and seem okay, but I hasten our pace before somebody calls for a doctor. What a disappointment I'd be to them.

We step out of the shade of an oak tree. Dolores inspects my head where the bro punched it.

"The bruise is gone," she says.

But we both know that's not how bruises work.

April 24

After the first visit, I knew the doctor wasn't going to have an answer, so why return? As Maggie Nelson asks, "...why bother with diagnoses at all, if a diagnosis is but *a restatement of the problem?*"

Do we visit doctors for answers or for something else?

"I like to know that I'm not pioneering an inexplicable experience," writes Esmé Weijun Wang.

No, the doctor has no explanation, but I like that others have come to her with the same pain before me. Solidarity is no cure, but maybe a comfort.

April 29

...

I'm in the nude, half-propped up in Hildie's bed. All the lights are on, curtains open. I'm directly below an AC vent, but I'm not allowed a blanket.

Hildie rolls to-and-fro on her stool, sketching me from various angles. Sometimes she pulls out her phone and snaps a photo. She doesn't like to talk while she does this kind of work. The tip of her pencil scratches against the paper. The stool's wheels ratchet on the parquet floor.

I'm modeling for a painting, her reinterpretation of Raphael's *Ezekiel's Vision*. I looked up the original. A clichéd figure of the Christian deity hovers among a heavenly host. Angels and pudgy cherubs. A bull and lion, both sprouting wings for symbolic reasons. Pink silk conceals the god from the waist down.

I asked why I had to be naked.

"Because I want to paint your balls," said Hildie, and I really couldn't argue with that.

No jokes now, though. Instead, a clinical gaze. I might as well be back at the doctor.

I fret over my physique. Since my migraines started, for six weeks, I haven't exercised. Whatever cut my muscles once showed has eroded. I don't want this version of my body to be painted. I want a younger version. A version who's just done fifty push-ups. The thought of doing push-ups throbs my head.

But I promised Hildie I'd pose for her months ago. My migraines hadn't been the subject then. She'd recruited me for another painting. It seems longer ago than months.

Hildie's gray cat, Hildie II, stalks by. He always hisses if I get close. I worry he'll attack me in a vulnerable area.

I've been tilting my head at a weird angle, down and to the right. My arms are raised halfway to signaling a touchdown. My shoulder muscles singe.

Hildie lives and paints on the first floor an old Victorian she rents near the downtown Kroger. Folks stroll by the broad window. If somebody looked in, I'd wave. There's nowhere to hide. I sip the beer Hildie gave me to relax. I set the beer down and re-assume my pose.

I think about the act of hiding. I think about vulnerability. My defenses have been removed. Parts that are usually concealed, made public. Here's my junk for all the world to see.

Pain works the same way. Pain expressed on my face is a peek at my hidden tissues. It's a map of the signals in my brain. Stars mark sites of interest. Tourists trek from site to site, gandering.

Pain is a loss of privacy.

Hilde stands and goes to the kitchen and comes back with a glass of water. She retakes the stool, but I can tell by her posture—back straight, shoulders spread—that she's done sketching.

I pull the bedsheet over my lap and sit up at a better angle. My neck unclenches. An ache pulses deep inside like a plucked string. I imagine a glacier breaking free, making the slow journey from my shoulder to my brain. I imagine KJ's stroke.

"You okay?" asks Hildie.

I must have winced.

"Same old pain," I say, even though this neck pain is newer.

Hildie flips through her sketchbook and shows a rough rendering of my penis. She grins extra wide, puckish. So much for professionalism.

"Lovely," I say.

"Dicks are hilarious," she says.

I laugh. There's indeed something comical about my disembodied dick.

"Raphael was scared of dicks," she says. "Or at least of his god's dick. But you can't be an artist if you're scared."

"Raphael did alright for himself."

"Maybe you have to be scared, then. Utterly terrified, but you do it anyway."

A man with gelled silver hair passes the window, pushing a shopping cart with one small plastic bag inside. You're not supposed to take the carts out of the Kroger parking lot.

"Being scared," I say. "I don't know if it's KJ or my migraines, but I'm scared all the time. I've never felt like that before. I'm hyperaware of my body and the ways it can break."

Hildie flips to another page. It's my whole naked self, ready to be fed grapes and fanned with palm fronds.

"But you do it anyway, right?" she says. "You live life."

I say, "I've been considering a *Keep on Truckin'* tattoo."

Hildie pencils in the tattoo on my sketch's shoulder.

"Since he died," she says, "I've been working so hard. Any free minute I turn to art. You know, he was always the first person I shared new ideas with. I used to call him and wake him up in the middle of the night. Less often once he started living with Dolores, but still sometimes. And he'd call me, too. When he died, my first selfish thought was about my art. Who would I share it with? But after a week, I found myself working harder, as if I had to create my art and his, both."

She shows me a sketch of my hand in detail. It's not open or closed. Somewhere in between. It could be in the act of opening or closing. Palm or fist to come.

"Maybe I'm trying to dull the pain," she says. "Keeping myself busy so I don't have to think about the loss. I can't paint and cry at the same time. But it feels different than that. This activity might sustain me. Is that the fear you're talking about? Am I scared I'll die before I finish the projects I wanna finish? Sure, of course, I'm scared of that. But I also think about how KJ would be so *pissed* at me if I didn't get shit done."

I try to remember a time before my migraines. I try to remember creativity. Pain superimposes itself over every memory. There was never a time before the hurt.

"Where are my jeans?" I ask.

Hildie rolls her stool over to the couch and retrieves them. I fish the pill fob out of my pocket and take three ibuprofens with a swig of beer. I sense Hildie watching me. No longer the gaze of the artist.

"We done?" I ask.

"I got what I need for today."

I slip on my boxers under the sheet and stand to put on my jeans. My t-shirt's wadded on the floor. My head throbs when I bend over to pick up the shirt. I stand straight and see stars.

Walking home, I pass the shopping cart, abandoned on the side of the street. If my head weren't aching, I'd return the cart to Kroger. That's what I tell myself.

The burning sensation is back on my lips. My tongue might be swollen. I'm short of breath by the time I get to my apartment. I take off my pants and climb into bed.

May 3
...

I should probably open a window. I haven't left my apartment all weekend. The room reeks of living in it.

I worry the hurt will reemerge. It sleeps in a corner of my head, a primordial monster. I tiptoe past it. I move in a wide circle around myself.

I can't tell if a migraine is coming or not anymore. They sometimes come without auras. My early warning system has busted. If I'm not sure if one is coming, then one's always coming. All time before a migraine is the hurt winding up.

An afternoon thunderstorm passes through Savannah. This could be any spring afternoon. I watch for flashes of lightning and count seconds till the thunder. The count never reaches one.

The sky is a wall of gray. The rain is another wall, also gray.

Today, I don't wait for the corgi to talk to me. I talk to him first.

"Hey, man." I say.

The corgi wiggles on the paper but doesn't respond. Can a drawing go out in the rain?

"I'm not scared of the rain," says the corgi in KJ's voice.

"What about lightning?"

"Of course I'm scared of lightning."

The corgi steps from the paper and goes to my kitchen. He gets a beer from the fridge.

"Most of all," he says, "I hate the pressure change. You're not supposed to *feel* the sky."

He sits on the sofa and tips the bottle up to his mouth and laps at the beer with his tongue. I wonder what a beer bottle for dogs would look like. Should I pour it into a bowl for him?

He sets the beer on the coffee table and stands on his hind legs.

"We better get going," he says.

I follow him out into the storm. I don't think to bring an umbrella. The wind whips the rain in from the side, so an umbrella wouldn't have been much use, anyway. A flash of lightning. Less than a second to the thunder. The hairs on my arms raise. The hair on my head is matted flat.

The rain is cooler than the air temperature. It's fallen from so high. It's been carried here from a faraway, cold place.

Lightning flashes. No time before the thunder. The wind and rain roar white noise.

"Is the lightning in the clouds from the start?" shouts the corgi. "Or does it emerge within the storm? I prefer to think that it's been there all along. That we can look at a cloud in Nebraska and predict where the lightning will strike here."

"Based on the accuracy of the local forecast," I say, "I don't think we ever really know what's coming."

"But we know it'll storm almost every afternoon through mid-summer. We don't know today for sure, but we know this season. Maybe that's enough. Maybe the universe is telling us that knowing specifics doesn't matter."

We turn left on Oglethorpe Avenue. The gnarly oak trees in the median drip fat drops of water. They're machines designed to merge small droplets into bigger ones.

My clothes cling all over. You can see the shallow contours of my arms and chest. My muscles are slack. The ancient athletic shorts I usually only wear around the apartment reveal the shape of my package. I might as well be nude.

We cross MLK Street and pass beyond downtown proper. We trudge up the ramp to the suspension bridge. The bridge is named after an old-timey racist, so most people call it simply *The Bridge*. At least people who aren't assholes.

My thighs burn with the ascent. Cars speed past and spray us with water. A cargo ship steams into port. It looks too tall to fit below the bridge. The bridge is higher than it looks.

The suspension cables are painted white. Standing next to one I realize how big it is, the pale trunk of a primordial tree. I could climb inside with room to spare. Assuming it's hollow. Rain flows down the cable in a slick.

The air fizzes with static. My skin feels infested.

Lightning explodes straight overhead, claiming half the sky. A thousand branches. A tree made of shattered glass. The trunk strikes the top of the suspension tower. A blue sphere shimmers there. The thunderclap quakes the bridge. The road falls away. I hover mid-air. The road rises back up and slaps my feet. My soles sting and then numb instantly. I hug the cable, but it's too broad to grip.

The cars in the center of the bridge tumble over the guardrail. One driver honks their horn mid-plummet. Sick thuds into the water, splashes like cotton balls.

The corgi peers over the railing.

"Just imagine," he says, "a storm carrying this moment for thousands of miles."

The shape of the lightning bolt superimposes on my vision. Among the spokes sparkle phosphenes. A blind spot grows over the sky and the bridge and the river.

I'm back in my apartment, as dry as ash. I take a bunch of ibuprofens and lie down. Outside, lightning flashes. The flashes happen inside my head at the same time.

The corgi is back on the sheet of paper. The paper blurs.

"Find it," he says.

To be honest, KJ's voice or not, I'm sick of this request.

The thunder is a steady rumble.

I close my eyes and watch the visions reel against the dark.

May 4
...

Let's set this straight. I know the corgi is an illusion. Or is the proper term *hallucination*? Most accurate might be *symptom*. Ninety-nine percent of the time he stays a silent sketch taped to the wall by my window. Black ink and yellow highlighter. He almost never speaks. When he does, it's cryptic.

But that doesn't mean he's wrong.

I believe there's a detail I'm missing, a misplaced object that needs to be found. There must be a reason KJ died. There are no freak accidents in the universe. Or else everything is a freak accident, which might as well be the same as the first case.

And there must be a reason for the migraines.

I've decided to say *the* migraines instead of *my* migraines. I don't want to think of them as an object I've chosen to own.

What's the connection between KJ's death and the pain? Grief is pain, and pain is grief. Could it all be in my head? Is it a joke to ask that about a headache?

A few years ago, I wrote a screenplay for a short film that KJ was supposed to animate. He did traditional hand-drawn cartoons. I pull the screenplay out of my file cabinet. The paper is crinkled and marked all over in green pen. The markings are from the night we sat at the coffee shop and went over the details.

KJ could write perfect little letters, neat as type.

He never finished the project, but I didn't expect him to. He was great at ideas. He was great at getting started. But he seldom pushed through to completion. I think that's why he stuck around Savannah and taught at the art college instead of moving to New York or LA. Not a lack of ambition, exactly, but admitting his ambition's extent.

I was excited by what KJ planned for this screenplay. It's the story of a moon the size of a softball that orbits a woman and falls in love with her. For the final scene, KJ sketched the moon and the woman in a starfield. The lines of constellations pulse around them like laser beams. He and Dolores had been dating for several months at that point. He was illustrating how he loved her.

I put the screenplay back in the file. KJ's little green letters march in front of my vision. They move like cartoon animals. I can hear the music that should go with them. Ba-dump, ba-dump. Ba-dump, ba-dump.

Sometimes I wonder if my brain knows more than I'm aware of. If that's the case, then the corgi is me telling myself there's some remainder that KJ left behind. I've subconsciously pieced together enough clues to know it exists, this relic. What exactly it is or where I might find it, that's beyond my comprehension.

I hope, but not out loud, that the corgi is more than just my brain misfiring. I hope it's the real KJ reaching out from the other side. The other side of what? I don't believe in that kind of shit. Instead, I hope it's a part of KJ that claimed a spot in my brain. It could be both my brain and KJ talking at the same time. My brain giving rise to his voice, his thoughts.

If it's him causing the pain, though, then we'll need to have a chat.

My Personal History of Pain
Part III
...

This is the story Hildie and I call *The Secret of the Roller Derby*. We recount it all the time, but I only now realize it also contains an element of pain. Not large, maybe barely worth including. But I've set a pattern, one I need to stick with whether I want to or not.

It was about six years ago, a Saturday afternoon, and there must have been some vibration to the ether, because Hildie and I texted each other at the exact same moment with the exact same question: *What are you up to?* She said Dolores was busy with a freelance gig. I said KJ was feeling run down. That alone should have told us something was up. KJ never passed on a chance to go out.

I met Hildie at Gallery, in that weird afternoon time, the gap between when we were always there in the morning and sometimes there at night. The faces of the other patrons were less familiar. Fanny packs and visors indicated tourism. Shirt necks limp with sweat. Even the baristas working the afternoon shift were ones we didn't know well, except for Chris. Chris was always working.

"Maybe somewhere else," said Hildie.

Somewhere else always meant a bar, so we strolled to Pinkie's and ordered a shot and a beer each. Sunlight came in around the edges of the blinds, maybe the first time in my hundred thousand visits I noticed there were windows connecting the inside of the bar to the outside world. The AC unit over the door burped humid air.

More tourists here, too, of course. They're inescapable. Hildie chatted up a couple beside her, from Ohio, always from

Ohio, and offered recommendations for restaurants, the insider recs, not the place run by the TV chef or the ones in City Market that pretend to be fancy. We never recommend our favorite Mexican place, though. Locals only.

The tourists cleared out over the course of an hour, and it was just me and Hildie and the lone bartender, who disappeared at intervals for smoke breaks. Hildie and I weren't talking, having just seen each other that morning, our stores of news and gossip and quotes from things we'd read or watched exhausted. She went to the restroom. I sipped my warming beer.

Hildie returned but didn't take her seat. She pulled me up by the elbow, dumped my beer in a to-go cup, and led me outside.

"We going somewhere?" I asked.

"Poster by the can," she said. "The roller derby is starting right now."

We trekked the few blocks from Pinkie's to the Civic Center, a 70s-vintage, beige-bricked assemblage of boxes, one half sports arena, the other concert halls. We paid the five-dollar admission fee and entered to the sound of staticky punk rock squawking from the arena's shitty speakers. The lower-level bleachers were full, so we found a clear spot in the suicide seats, an arch of floor taped off just beyond the rounded end of the track. The ref blew a shrill whistle, and the first lap went live.

Skaters zoomed right in front of us, falls and scuffles, a shoving match on wheels. A pleasant buzz settled in from my drinks. The rules of roller derby started coming back to me. The fans were into it, jeering the opponents from Charleston. Whether that was because they were any opponent or specifically Charlestonians wasn't clear, a rival team and a rival city, Savannah's soberer, less-fun-at-a-party sister.

The next lap neared us. The jammer for Savannah battled in the middle of the pack, trying to break free. A Charlestonian threw a cheap high shove. The jammer's skates flew out in front of her, tripping half the pack, all of them sprawling in our direction. The person in front of me fell back on their elbows, one of which found the top of my foot through the thin canvas of my Chuck. I yelped, kind of a pathetic sound.

Rubbing my foot ineffectually through my shoe, my attention drifted over the mass of skaters before me, disentangling limbs from each other. Think spaghetti. A cluster of musty sweat smells. Helmets and knee pads and skates clacking. A slow process to becoming individuals again.

I scanned the crowd and found KJ and Dolores's faces, but of course that couldn't be right. Here they were, though, sitting together on a day when they both said they were unavailable. They didn't watch the match, intent on each other, and—no, this couldn't be right, this must be some pair that looked like our friends—they held hands, fingers interlocked in the romantic way. No mere squeeze of comfort, camaraderie, platonic closeness. The whirring of my brain had made me forget the smarting of my foot. My hand still rested atop my shoe, as if my foot were someone else's hand. Someone else with whom I was clearly on a date.

"Hildie," I said.

She was back into the action of the derby and ignored me. The skaters had reached the other end of the track.

"Hildie," I repeated, tapping her leg.

"Huh?" she said and looked at me. "What's your face doing?"

I could sense an unfamiliar expression, a mix of emotions twisting muscles into new configurations.

I pointed at our friends.

She looked for a moment, processing.

"Oh," she said. "I guess that makes sense."

"How the hell does this make sense?"

"Haven't you noticed the two of them bailing more often than they used to? We've all gotten busier with work and shit, but I wondered what was up. Now we know. Those two are fucking."

Not just a date, then. I hadn't been able to take the thought any further. All feeling left my face. I was outside of my head, on the track, going round and round and round.

"Are you okay with that?" she asked.

"I will be," I said.

"I'm not okay, though, with them hiding it from us. I think it's time we exploded their little secret."

So, that's how we ended up leaving the derby early and waiting outside the Civic Center, leaning on one of the big brick columns by the exit. When KJ and Dolores came out, we were there, grinning imps amidst our new knowledge. Hildie's smile seemed real. Mine felt forced. The couple—because it was clear that's what they were—froze in the doorway, blocking the flow of traffic, summoning spattered complaints. They approached us sheepishly. Hildie didn't wait. She closed the gap and pulled them into a hug. A beat later, I joined. I didn't much feel like hugging, but I did feel like I needed to hold something. It was maybe the first seismic shift of my young adult life. I wanted to be happy for them, but even today, in retrospect, I don't know exactly what I felt. My eyes burned with pending tears. I held them in and kept the discomfort to myself.

May 5

...

The Middle Scots poet William Dunbar, working in the service of James IV of Scotland, following a migraine, wrote this apology to his patron:

> To dyt thocht I begowthe to dres,
> The sentence lay full evill till find,
> Unsleipit in my heid behind,
> Dullit in dulnes and distres.

Translated by scholar Jenni Nuttall: "...though I tried to begin to write, the sense of it lurked very hard to find, deep down sleepless in my head, dulled in dullness and distress."

When it comes to narratives of illness, Arthur W. Frank observes, "The story is both interrupted and it is about interruption."

Here we are trying to write about a thing that wants to thwart our writing.

May 7

...

I spent yesterday in the throes of a vicious migraine, reduced to gasps whenever I moved. I thought I was dying. There's a term for this I google later: angor animi. But I woke up this morning, worn but breathing. I found an unsent text to Dolores on my phone: "I'm sorry."

My inner parts have been rubbed over with sandpaper. The surfaces of my mouth are inflamed.

So, it seemed like a good idea to come out for a drink. I meet Dolores and Hildie at Pinkie's. We order beers and take the four-seater booth by the door.

The AC unit over the door chugs futilely, the little engine that couldn't quite. The vinyl of the seat is sticky with humidity.

Dolores tenses. She sets her beer down. I glance back and there's the bro who punched me. I refused to fight him the first time, but I decide I might now.

He's bigger than me. He could break my bones if he got a grip. I convince myself I'm quick and stronger than I look. I convince myself to fight dirty.

The bro stops at the end of our table. He directs his eyes to the grimy barroom floor. His body is surrounded by a sweet, floral aura, a little strong but not so bad.

"Listen," says the bro. "I'm sorry about the other night. I was being an asshole. When I came back to apologize to the bartender, he told me about your situation." He finally raises his eyes to Dolores. "About your fiancé." He makes eye contact with me. "Your friend."

Matt comes up behind him. I think he's going to ask the bro to leave us alone, but Matt delivers a round of shots. Jeezus, it's Jägermeister. Of all the peace offerings. Matt deposits the shots on the table.

The bro continues, "Sometimes me and my buddies roll into town looking to cause some trouble. We didn't used to be like that. But we lost friends on our last tour in Afghanistan. Since then, hitting somebody or taking a hit is the only way to get my head to quiet down. I don't want to hurt anybody. Or I do want to hurt somebody, but I know I'm still okay if I can hold myself back. A couple punches, and that's it."

He rubs his close-cropped hair. He looks back at me.

"I'm sorry about that. You were talking some shit, so I thought you were down for a fight. I did that wrong. I don't understand what's happening. Ever since we got back..."

And now the bro is crying. I survey the bar, embarrassed on his behalf, but nobody's watching.

Dolores picks up a shot glass and raises it to the bro.

"To second chances," she says.

The bro claims his shot, and Hildie hers. I'm the last. I don't want to toast, but not because I'm mad. Not because of the punch. I don't want to toast him because he dumped all *his* shit on *us*. Ours is a table full of loss. There's no room to add more.

In the end, I raise my glass. We all repeat Dolores's toast. We throw back the viscous liquid. I grimace at the licorice aftertaste. It'll ruin whatever else I drink tonight.

Dolores points to the empty seat beside Hildie. "Join us?"

The bro sits. Hildie studies her empty shot glass.

She asks, "So, what exactly the hell is happening here?"

I laugh. The tension melts. I can sense my blood pressure returning to normal. It's weird to be aware of my blood.

"This dude punched me in the head," I say, "but it's okay because Dolores punched him first."

I note the bro's earlobe is no longer swollen.

"Now we're all friends?" asks Hildie.

"Looks that way," says Dolores. She stacks the empty shot glasses one in the other.

"What's your name?" asks Hildie.

"Ollie," says the bro.

"Army?"

He nods.

She slips her arm through the crook of his elbow. Jeezus, she's going to take him home. I can never tell where Hildie's taste in partners lies.

"Where are you from?" she asks.

The conversation expands from there. The bro ceases being *the bro* and becomes Ollie. I learn all sorts of facts about him. Hildie is practically an interrogator. The Jäger goes to my head and I forget all I learn as quickly as it comes.

Dolores doesn't say much, but she pays attention. I try to figure out exactly where her attention is directed. I think I see what she's seeing. Here's a person who was broken moments ago, now resuming life. Ollie is a summary of the healing process.

We drink more. The locked gates in my brain open and I find myself liking Ollie. He's pretty different from how he presents. Maybe I owe him an apology for assuming who he was from a single encounter.

Getting punched precludes apology.

When we call it a night, Hildie leaves with Ollie, as anticipated. In a way, I'm glad. I'm glad to have a friend I know well enough to know what's coming.

Tomorrow morning I'll make a joke to Hildie about her smelling like Ollie's cologne.

May 8
...

I don't make my joke to Hildie because when she arrives, fucking Ollie arrives with her. I'm already feeling gross this morning. Hungover, yes, but also my sinuses have been stuffed since last night. The pressure squeezes the migraine spot.

Ollie orders a cappuccino, which isn't what I expect.

Dolores comes in. She doesn't show surprise at Ollie. I realize Hildie asked her in advance if it was alright to bring him to Breakfast Club. I'm miffed Hildie didn't ask me, too.

Ollie goes to the front of the shop to snag a copy of the local alt weekly newspaper.

"Really?" I whisper to Hildie.

She shushes me. She grins in a way she hasn't since before KJ died. I shush.

Ollie sits on Hildie's right, on the opposite side of us from KJ's stool. Ollie does the crossword puzzle and drinks his cappuccino. He has nice arms, I notice, and nice other muscles. His t-shirt strains to contain him.

I don't want to see handsome Ollie, and not looking at him forces my focus to the vacant stool where KJ should be. I didn't realize until now how I've avoided it. My coffee is long since cold, but I take careful sips like it's hot.

I have my computer open. I've had it open and in front of me for the weeks since KJ died. I type, but it's gibberish. No words string together. Sentences won't form. Forward motion stalls. I never save the documents.

There's no whiff of Ollie's cologne today. No unfamiliar odors at all. I realize he showered at Hildie's. He's used her soap and her shampoo, so their scents match.

Hildie talks to him, but I can't hear what she's saying. The ocean is in my ears. I flash back to KJ's memorial at the beach.

The phosphenes appear. I welcome them. Little stars, old friends. They're familiar when the counter at the coffee shop this morning is not.

A speck of light like a ding in a windshield flickers at the center of my sight. It grows, carving out a whole area of blindness.

The core of Ollie's face is gone, his head a donut of flesh. All the middle parts scooped out. I choke back a gasp. This is a nightmare vision. Sometimes the visions are benign. I might find them amusing if not for the pain I knew to follow. But this vision is a punch to the side of the head. I look away from Ollie, but everyone's face is hollowed.

I sneak out the pill fob. My elbow brushes Dolores. The pills ping the metal. A maraca. Dolores notices, stares at me. But I can't see her face, so I don't know if she's staring or not. Is this even Dolores? Everyone could have been replaced with someone else. A world of faceless alien monster ghoul demons.

I swallow all the pills from the fob. I chug the rest of my cold coffee. It tastes extra bitter. Time moves slowly. Time rushes by. Time is bullshit.

A fierce burning consumes my throat. My tongue is larger than my whole head. How does it stay tucked inside? My skin itches all over.

I can see faces again, but they're far away. Ollie has almost completed the crossword. Is he a crossword puzzle savant? Or has time fucked itself even worse? My heart beats rapid-fire, filling my ears with noise.

All of a sudden, I'm sure I'm dying. Angor animi. I'm an angry animal. I'm angry about how soon I'm going to die. I know death with a certainty I've never known anything before.

I can't draw breath. I stand up to walk outside. Fresh air, the miracle cure. I get dizzy and brace myself on the counter. I slip off the counter and fall to my ass on the floor. Everyone's around me asking if I'm alright. Ollie takes charge. Ollie's been trained as a medic. Of course he has.

People are talking all at once. Even when they talk one at a time, I process it as an unintelligible stew. Single words emerge to the surface. Swollen. Panting. Ollie says anaphylaxis. Chris is on the phone. He says ambulance, emergency.

Later, I wake in the back of the ambulance. I smell the tang of vomit on my shirt. A stinging ache in my thigh. A migraine in my head.

Later, in the hospital, Dolores is there by the bed. She's been crying. I'm so mad at myself for doing this to her. I want to apologize, but I can't control the workings of my mouth. My tongue no longer feels fat. I'm not sure it's there at all. Maybe they had to remove it to keep me from choking.

I muster the energy to say *I'm sorry*, but it only comes out as a croak.

DIARY TWO

May 17
...

Holy shit, hospitals are expensive.

May 18

Turns out I've developed an allergy to ibuprofen. The reaction can get worse each time you use a drug. I reached the tipping point at the coffee shop. That was a couple weeks ago. If I'd been at home alone, I would have died.

I don't voice that detail to Dolores or Hildie. They're smart enough to figure it out on their own.

I haven't had a full migraine since it happened. I want to thank my body for giving me this break. But that's some Stockholm Syndrome shit, isn't it? Thanks for taking a break from kidnapping my life, body.

Fuck you body and fuck you brain and fuck you.

I'm back at the doctor. Same lobby. Same illness everywhere. The nurse calls my name, and I'm lost in the back of the office as soon as I step through the door. I swim the fluorescent sea. The nurse takes my vitals. My life converted to numbers. The nurse leaves.

The doctor knocks and comes in. She has all the info from the hospital. She says vaguenesses meant to comfort me. She says no more NSAIDs. She lists off the various types. She prescribes a migraine drug, a triptan. It works differently, she says. She could make up outrageous lies and I'd believe her. I pick up my new prescription from the pharmacy and leave.

I cross the street and go back to my office. The edit suite is dark. I bump into the file cabinet. I wiggle the mouse, and the monitors reignite. On my desk, flowers wilt in a Garfield coffee mug, a makeshift vase. The card with the flowers says *Welcome back*. I interpret that phrase as broadly as possible.

My job is just a job, but today I'm grateful for it. The routine. The familiar.

I'm OK when the monitors start to ripple. I have the new drug, but I don't take it. The directions say to take it at the first sign, but I'm trigger shy.

How bad does the pain need to be before I risk death? How bad until I contemplate it?

After work, I head straight home. The pain's held out. The ripples never grew to waves.

Thank you, body.

I've barely left my apartment since I got back from the hospital. I've barely walked or lifted an object or used a muscle.

I go to bed early and wake up late and repeat the cycle.

May 19
...

From *Sick* by Porochista Khakpour: "The body is asking for something, and drugs deliver something, but rarely that thing the body needs."

Is there a hole in the body with a specific shape into which a cure can be fit? Or is an ambiguous *something* as close as we can get? *Needs* too strong a word?

Is it the body asking, or me, the mind? And if it's me, how is that different from prayer?

Every pill a psalm.

May 20

...

Hildie swings by mid-morning. She orders me to shower and stands in the bathroom doorway. The swish of the water messes with my vision. The tub flattens to two dimensions. I'm a stickman in a sketch.

Hildie chats while I lather up. I miss most of what she says. She doesn't seem to expect a response. She stays there when I step out and towel off. I'm self-conscious. I don't care at all.

As soon as I'm dressed, she clamps me in a hug. Steam and soap scent cling to her hair.

"Let's get going," she says.

It might as well be summer. The heat, the mugginess. Any time after April can pass for summer in Savannah. Hildie leads us east. We enter the less familiar part of downtown, old houses and secluded squares. No tourists.

I catalog the things that might kill me while we walk: cars going the wrong way on one-way streets, lightning strikes, flash floods, accidentally taking an ibuprofen.

My own body.

We pass the little house I always like, freestanding but no bigger than my apartment. A plaque on the front declares the house is over two hundred years old. The shutters are painted purple.

"I've been sitting in your seat at Breakfast Club," says Hildie. "If I don't, Dolores stares at the empty space between us the whole time."

I mmhmm.

We turn south on Broad Street, near the old pink shotgun house Hildie used to rent, and cut across the baseball field by the elementary school. The red clay of the infield is hard packed. Sere grass.

Ahead of us, the dog park. Barks and yips. KJ and I used to come here all the time just to hang out. We both adore dogs, but our leases forbid them.

Hildie and I lean on the fence and watch. The dogs scamper in packs that break apart and reform as new packs. Eddies in an ocean.

A border collie streaks after a thrown tennis ball. Other dogs run for it, too, but the border collie outpaces them.

Some of the owners keep an eye on us. As if we're brazen dog-nappers plotting a heist.

I read patterns in the dogs' movements. I almost make sense of it before sense slips away. If you watched enough dogs for enough time, eventually you'd invent ballet.

A kindly hound saunters up and sniffs at us and accepts a pat.

Hildie pushes off the fence. I follow her back across the baseball diamond. Orange dust kicks up from the infield.

She says, "KJ loved little dogs with ugly faces."

It's true. If one walked by the coffee shop window in the morning, he'd sketch it on a napkin. The corgi was far from the first dog drawing he gave me.

Hildie says, "She needs you, you know."

I don't respond.

"Dolores loved KJ, and I'm her best friend, but you're family. You're more family than her parents or sisters. She loves you in a way she didn't even love him."

A white dog with a droopy tail prances toward the dog park.

"You've been together as friends for your entire adult lives. You're the family she chose, but these last few weeks, she's lost you, too."

Hildie punches me in the shoulder. I nod to indicate I've been hearing her.

"I'm surprised you two never hooked up," she says. "I'm glad, but surprised."

"Not that I didn't try a couple times, way back when," I say.

"Then I'm glad you're hopelessly awkward. Because your friendship is so lovely. Sometimes I'm painting, and my hand is working on its own, and my brain goes off to wherever. When I think the word *beauty*, I think of you two. The friendship you've made and maintained. But you've both closed off since KJ died. She feels guilty for losing you your best friend, and you feel guilty that you brought them together only for her to lose him." She throws up her hands, a gesture at the universe. "Sorry for the amateur psychoanalysis."

I don't know if Hildie's right. Sure, the four of us are arguments in favor of the impermanence of family. I don't speak to mine. Hildie barely does. We all adopted each other, but the terms of the adoption were conditional. One of us would move away. One of us would move on. One of us would die.

Is there any arrangement that isn't conditional?

We cross Broad Street. Hildie halts in the middle and looks down. There's a dead squirrel, at least the remains of one, pancaked so flat the texture of the asphalt shows through. The poor critter has been unmade. The word *squirrel* shouldn't apply. Except for the intact tail, which sticks straight up, perpendicular to the road. Gross but hilarious.

Hildie pulls out her phone and snaps photos from several angles. Cars near us from either direction, but there's time before they arrive.

"In short," she says, hunched for a photo, "come back to Breakfast Club."

Hildie might not be right about everything, but this much I can do. The pain, the near-death, those I can ignore for an hour each morning. I don't know about family, but I know debt. I owe Dolores whatever time she needs.

The first car is almost here. Anxiety pumps in my bloodstream. Discomfort returns to the spot in my head. I pull Hildie up and out of the street.

My Personal History of Pain
Part IV
...

This is back when Hildie still rented the pink shotgun house on the east side of downtown, near the dog park, cinder blocks painted a Pepto color with black trim. She'd done it up nice inside, though. She had a knack for finding cool furnishings secondhand. She always had new art to display.

My house, Hildie had texted. *Come quick.*

What's up? texted Dolores.

Kitten was Hildie's one-word reply.

So it was with moderate disappointment that when we all arrived within a few minutes of each other, there was no kitten in her apartment, no cat, no animal that might be confused for a cat, no animal at all except one might assume the palmetto bugs that lived in the walls of every structure in Savannah.

The small living room smelled of pot, and Hildie produced a joint like a magic trick, suddenly pinched in her fingers where nothing had been before. I worried that *kitten* was a new term for marijuana and that the cool kids' slang had once again outpaced me. We each took a drag. Hildie led us to her back door. On the other side of the rusting screen was a closet-sized courtyard. Weeds struggled from the seams in bricks slick with a green-black slime. Ivy grew up the privacy fence, consuming it entirely. A small metal table and chair bunched in the corner.

"I didn't know you had a yard," said KJ.

"Such as it is," said Hildie.

"I think it's cute," said Dolores. "I'd read out there every day if it was mine."

We looked out the door for a while longer, the silence stretching into weirdness.

"So," said KJ, "something about a kitten?"

"Just wait for it," said Hildie.

A breeze shifted shadows across the ivy, ripples and oscillations and moments when the whole leafy wall erupted in random flutters like applause. I could almost pick out patterns that would make sense of the whole thing.

At the bottom of the ivy, through a hidden gap in the fence, the smallest face appeared, followed by the clumsy body of a kitten, all gray, gangly, awkward in its movements. It puttered to a saucer filled with kibble. When the kitten raised its face, crumbs clung to its nose and whiskers.

"Well, that's the cutest thing ever," said KJ.

The kitten froze at the sound of his voice but soon returned to its meal.

"I want to bring it inside," whispered Hildie, "but it won't let me get close."

"And we're here to what," I said, "tackle it?"

"You're my think tank to figure out how to trap it. I made a net from a dowel and a coat hanger and a pillow case, but if I'm out there, the kitten won't come. I've never seen any siblings or its mom, so I think it's alone, poor tiny baby."

The kitten finished eating and left the way it came. We smoked some more and schemed, and in the end devised a plan familiar to anybody who grew up watching Saturday morning cartoons: a cardboard box propped on a stick over the saucer, the stick tied a string so we could activate the trap from inside. We set up the contraption and waited. And waited some more. We sat on the cheap vinyl of the kitchen floor. Any bit of bare flesh stuck to the surface and released with a shmack. We moved from smoking to beer. We chatted about every topic imaginable. Time blurred and stretched and disappeared altogether.

We almost missed the kitten's return. It was KJ who spotted it, a small gray shadow in the deeper grays of dusk. The kitten made a hesitant lap around the box, sniffing underneath, and boldly entered. Dolores yanked the string, and damn if the trap didn't work, cartoon physics holding up in the real world. We ran outside and surrounded the box on our knees. The kitten's tiny, pathetic mews echoed within.

Hildie and KJ tilted up one end of the box, and I reached underneath. Its whole body, squirmy and warm, fit in my hands. Its mewing grew to screeches. Dolores cooed and soothed it as I carried it inside. The kitten went quiet, reared its oversized head back, and then bit me. I remember the feel of its tiny needle teeth sinking in, a sensation more like sickness than pain. I hissed in through my teeth.

Hildie brought in the box from outside. Dolores placed a folded towel in the bottom. I set the kitten down, almost dropping it, just as it seemed ready to strike again.

"Careful," said KJ, smacking my shoulder.

My hand had two tiny specks of blood, perfect red orbs. I flexed my grip.

"Hope you're up to date on your tetanus shot," said KJ.

"Hope that thing doesn't have rabies," I said.

"It's not a thing," said Hildie, "It's my cat."

"You're keeping it?" I asked.

She reached in and stroked the kitten's head with the back of her fingers. I'm not sure the kitten even noticed. It made trembling orbits of the box's edge. Dolores and KJ took turns petting it.

"It looks shocked," he said.

"What else could it be?" said Dolores. "What would any of us be? One second you're enjoying a free meal, and then your whole understanding of the universe upends." She leaned over and talked in a baby voice. "But you're a brave little thing, aren't you? Sorry, not a *thing*. I think you're going to be just fine."

"Everyone," said Hildie, grandly sweeping her arm toward the kitten, "Please allow me to introduce you to the honorable Hildie II."

"What if it's a boy cat?" I asked

"What if it is?"

I reached in to pat Hildie II, but it hissed, and I yanked my hand away.

May 21
...

I'm starting to get saints and visionaries. When the hallucinations come, I don't think it's me that's changed. I believe with religious fervor it's the world changing around me. There's not a glitch in my eyes, I'm simply seeing what I missed before. I experience wonder and humility and exultation. I almost feel special. What to do with that feeling?

Lewis Carrol probably had migraines. Virginia Woolf. Charles Darwin.

Ezekiel, Freud, and Elvis, all famous enough to know by a single name.

Serena Williams. I can't imagine doing anything during the pain, much less winning Wimbledon.

Did these people overcome their migraines or gain essential wisdom from them? Could Lewis Carroll have written *Alice in Wonderland* if he hadn't endured the acid-trip of an aura first? Do we remember him only because of his trauma?

That path to fame certainly paid off for Jesus. One thing religious figures cherish as much as visions is suffering.

I'm jotting these thoughts down in the diary when Dolores joins me at the coffee shop. I haven't seen her since the hospital. We've texted. I told her I needed rest. I needed to sleep in.

We hug. I lean into her or she leans into me. We release. She sits at the counter, and the last two weeks are erased.

I think of all we've lately erased.

I expect a blind spot to form in my vision, but for once I can see fine.

I finish my cup of coffee and order a refill. A second cup can help chase away the creeping depression. Later, I'll pay for it with a crash. I marvel at the delicacy of my system. It's a miracle there aren't more imbalances, more mysterious pains.

Hildie comes in with Ollie. I notice the haunting behind Ollie's stare. He seldom makes eye contact, and that's what lets you spy the ghosts slinking in the corners. He spreads out the newspaper crossword and sets to work.

Is he part of this family now? Will he be here in a year? In ten? It's like he's auditioning to replace KJ. I don't want to think of him that way, but I can't help it. All I know about this guy are his fist and his hauntings.

I greet the first phosphenes as old friends. I've got the new pills with me, the triptans. I'm nervous to try one.

Pills are little pebbles and some of them kill you.

I take the fob from my pocket and shake out a pill. Dolores watches me from one side and Hildie from the other. Ollie, that kindly bastard, focuses on his crossword. I swallow the pill with the dregs of my coffee. My heart rate surges, blossoming the phosphenes. It's odd to be scared to swallow.

I pretend to write. I want Dolores to know I'm not going to keel over. I want to be sure of that myself before I go home alone. I have no idea what I'm typing at this point. The laptop screen blurs. I touch type, but I never learned how. I'll clean it up later. I'll finish telling the story.

The word *story* implies a shape.

I'm supposed to lie down after taking the pill. Stay cool. Bubbles pop and fizz in my brain. I pack up and leave. I hope I said a proper goodbye.

I lie on my sofa and turn on *Naruto* with the sound low. I have half-lucid dreams featuring the show's characters. I go on ninja adventures, but also sometimes grocery shopping with Naruto at the downtown Kroger.

Pain prods behind my eye, a burglar jiggling doorknobs, one door always left unlocked.

The window AC unit kicks on and drowns out the TV's sound. I fly through a cosmic wormhole. Prismatic colors swoop past. Stars and nebulae and galaxies. I travel to the far corners of the universe.

The AC turns off and I'm back at Kroger with Naruto. KJ's corgi is there with us now, too. Our activities are slow and boring. This is the worst filler episode of *Naruto* ever.

The AC kicks back on. More starfields. Time stops or flows backward. If I travel fast enough through the wormhole, I'll return to the Big Bang. I'll have been there when it all began. Time and space are bullshit.

Later, I'm sitting up and alive. That doesn't sound like much, but it's everything. Instead of a lost day, I've lost a couple hours. I don't feel exactly right. I've resigned myself to wrongness.

I take out my phone and text Dolores, "Great to see you today!"

June 10

...

Our writing group meets at the Flannery O'Connor Childhood Home, a three-story townhouse-turned-museum on Lafayette Square. Flannery lived here as a kid. The cathedral looms out the front window. No wonder Flannery grew up extra Catholic.

It's almost time to start, but it's only me and Alison. We're set up in the long, narrow parlor. We sit on folding chairs because we aren't allowed to use the vintage furniture. Alison reads a paperback, cover curled over so I can't tell what book it is.

Sometimes we'll have twenty people, sometimes just one of us. Alison, Dolores, and I are the three remaining original members. We take turns leading sessions. I've missed the last couple months. Dolores has, too, and she's absent again.

A tour bus goes by outside. I can hear the amplified voice of the guide but can't make out her words. I sip weak tea from a mug with the Home's logo on it.

Alison closes the book and slips it in her bag.

"How are the migraines?" she asks.

Alison was an English major in undergrad but is a pediatrician by day. She works at the hospital. When I was there, she came and saw me. She doublechecked my charts. The kid in the next bed was one of her patients. He had a marble stuck in his nose. According to the kid's father, the marble was valuable.

"Two or three times a week," I say. "Always feels like one's about to start."

"Aura?" she asks.

"Usually, but it's the pain that gets me."

She nods. "Hence the ibuprofen."

In this moment, Alison exists in a space between friend and medical professional.

An antique lamp emits hazy light in the corner. An ethereal sphere glows around it.

"You know one of the strangest things about being a doctor?" she says. "Pain is never *the* subject. In all my years of medical school and internship and residency, I maybe sat in five hours of instruction on pain. It's the number one complaint that drives people to a doctor's office, but we see it as a symptom of something else. We don't address the pain directly. That's why some people have such negative experiences. They're concerned with the pain, but the doctor's concerned with an underlying cause, which can turn out not to be there, at least not in a clear way."

A silhouette rises up the front steps. I was hoping nobody would show. I'm not in the mood to discuss writing. I haven't written any stories worth discussing.

The door opens and Dolores comes in. Alison jumps up and hugs her. It's probably the first time they've seen each other since KJ's memorial. Dolores takes one of the folding chairs. It squeaks. We're spread around the parlor in a broad triangle.

"Only the three of us?" asks Dolores.

"Like old times," I say.

"We've been sitting in this room for a decade," she says.

We fall silent at that. I remember the group's initial meeting. I sat on the floor because there were more writers than seats. How many faces have passed through the group since then? How many of those faces have I forgotten?

Dolores and Alison catch up. Alison skillfully elides the sensitive questions. She's used to skirting the topic of death. That's ninety percent of bedside manner.

No one else shows up after fifteen minutes, so we decide to call it. We fold up the chairs and stack them in the kitchen. Dolores rightens a painting gone crooked on the wall. She adjusts the lace curtains.

Dolores and Alison wait outside while I set the alarm. I lock the door and bid the ghosts goodnight.

The lamps in the square emit orange light. Spheres shine in the haze around them. I can sense my eyes adjusting.

A couple sits on the edge of the fountain. Water splashes. The sound sends ripples across the world. The sound irritates me. I'm irrationally mad at it. This sound I've heard a hundred times. A sound so like a shower I can't say it's different.

Dolores produces a flask from her backpack. Inside will be whiskey. I worry that she had it so handy on a random Tuesday night. She passes the flask around as we walk. I take a healthy gulp and wait for the alcohol to silence my concerns. I close my eyes and when I open them, I'm surprised to be farther along.

"Are you seeing a therapist?" asks Alison.

Dolores waggles the flask. "Other than this one?"

"Yes, other than that one."

"Yeah," says Dolores, "I've been seeing somebody."

This is news to me. We should all have doctor friends for important questions everybody else is too timid to ask.

We move slowly down Abercorn Street. This route runs alongside Colonial Cemetery. I once heard a tour guide say the cemetery used to be larger. Wherever you walk in the city, it's over the graves of dead colonists.

I position myself between Dolores and the cemetery. As if I can block the view. As if I can interrupt the associations. We leave the cemetery behind.

We emerge into the bright lights of Broughton Street. Dolores looks like Dolores for the first time in a while.

We end up in Johnson Square. An obelisk rises dead center. Monument designers love a fucking obelisk. Twin fountains burble on either side of the square. The surface of the world is a disturbed puddle.

Why are all the lamps orange?

Insects swarm in the light. I try to follow a single bug but lose it immediately. People swat in front of their faces. In every direction, there's someone swatting. This is a Southern springtime. Maybe there's only one bug moving so fast it's simultaneously everywhere. I like the idea that we're all experiencing the same annoyance.

Couples dot the square. Sitting on benches, walking hand in hand, leaning against an old oak tree, practically grinding.

It's this reminder of her lost life, not the cemetery, that I should be worried about for Dolores. When they were younger and first together, I'm sure she and KJ had public displays that made these seem tame.

Squatting atop a wicker mat, an old man sells fake roses folded from palmetto fronds. He extends one to every couple that passes. He's out here daily selling roses, a weathered obelisk.

Dolores goes up to the peddler and buys a rose. She holds it out for me and Alison to inspect. The technique impresses. There are a hundred twists and bends. I wouldn't know where to start to craft it.

Alison says goodnight. She lives across town in a neighborhood that requires driving to get there.

Dolores and I claim a bench. To a passerby, we'd look like a couple. She unfolds the rose, starting with the knot at the end that keeps it all together. She pinches the frond between her thumb and finger to straighten it. It won't completely straighten.

I swat at a bug.

I think of the corgi's command, to find it, and I wonder if this is what he meant.

We drain the whiskey. Dolores finishes unfolding the rose. No sense has been revealed in the space where the rose once was. I'm no closer to kenning how it was made.

I walk Dolores back to her apartment. We share an awkward goodnight, as if we haven't known each other for years and years.

I wander through Forsyth Park. It's after hours, so I'm breaking the law. I circle the fountain. I read a guidebook that said the fountain is the most photographed site in Savannah.

The fountain was assembled from a kit ordered from a catalog.

The water splashes louder in the dark. My vision ripples. Or is it the world rippling?

I experience the pain before it arrives.

I'm still carrying the palmetto frond, bent and mangled. When did Dolores give it to me? I lean over the railing to toss the frond into the fountain. The frond doesn't get there. Not even close. The aerodynamics are all wrong. I shut my eyes and make a wish.

June 20

Doctors write about the "constellation" of a patient's migraine symptoms. I like that. I like that it implies pieces held together by imaginary lines. My fingers tingle or my tongue. My vision goes bad or I hear things that aren't there. The hurt, the hurt, the hurt.

Connect all these dots, and you have me.

Since KJ died, I think of friendships as a constellation, too. I can't define how I was a friend to him without defining how I'm a friend to Dolores and Hildie, how they were friends with him, and how they're friends with each other.

We were quadrilateral. Now one side has gone missing.

Stars sputter out, but that happens on a not-human scale. Constellations are supposed to last. They guide ships at sea and herald seasons.

I imagine the Big Dipper losing a star, spilling out the Milky Way.

But I don't feel a new image forming within our friendship, only loss. The shape of the structure, this fragile triangle, teeters close to collapse. All the connections strain. We're the same people we used to be. We're all completely different.

I hope that friendship is more than obligation.

I hope that all shapes settle into a stable state.

How many constellations can I recognize? Not many. Orion. The Dippers. Cassiopeia. The Pleiades, seven stars called the Seven Sisters, six of which my eyes are good enough to pick out on a clear night.

June 25
...

All dates are approximations.

I could cut the squares out of a calendar and rearrange them and end up with basically the same thing. Shuffled cards. A shifting grid. Those little plastic puzzles where you slide the pieces around to make a picture. The numbers and the days refuse to line up.

Time is bullshit.

June 26
...

My fingertips tingle. There's a thrum underneath my skin. I take a triptan. I've learned that taking one usually summons the corgi to come to life. This feels like a magic trick. Nothing up my sleeve.

I sit in my chair and watch the sketch. My neck is a frond, too frail to support the growing weight of my head.

The corgi twitches on the page. Just a wave of his paw at first. His slumber is as deep as death. It takes him a while to get moving.

He steps out of the paper and goes into the bathroom. He doesn't bother to close the door. I guess dogs are used to pooping in front of people. The toilet flushes. The sink splashes on and off. The corgi comes out shaking his paws to finish drying them.

"Where to today?" I ask.

I'm excited. I've barely left my apartment except for work. It's not that I don't want to do things. I'm scared that doing things will trigger a migraine. More than fear, this has evolved into instinct.

The window AC unit kicks on. The sound distorts the corgi. He stands in the middle of a streaking starfield.

He climbs into the cockpit of a spaceship. The ship is sleek silver, a bulbous rocket. Swooping fins adorn the tail. Sexy, like old illustrations before we knew how rockets would really look. Think Buck Rogers.

I climb into the ship's back seat. The clear, seamless dome of the cockpit closes over us. Air hisses. My ears pop with the pressurization.

We zoom into the starfield. I catch glimpses of planets. Mars and Jupiter and Saturn, like illustrations of the solar system in a grade school textbook. There goes tiny Pluto.

We enter open space. The stars are all around us. All around the stars is a void.

A constellation needs blackness for its shape as much as light.

The Milky Way appears as a lazy river in the sky. Everything is sky.

G-forces smush me to the seat as the ship turns. The seat is some sort of space-age foam. We aim for a single bright star.

The corgi is so quiet today. I've been having trouble recalling the timbre of KJ's voice.

The star grows ahead of us. It's surrounded by a smoldering disc of gas and dust. A new star system in the process of being born. Within the disc spin eddies, planets in progress.

"Where are we?" I ask the corgi.

"Far away from all you know," he says in KJ's voice. It's hard to hear him over the ship's humming innards.

The spaceship dips into the outer edge of the disc. The gases react with the hull, surrounding us in aurora, waves of purples and greens.

I want to stay here forever.

Bolts of red streak past us from behind. I twist in my seat. Another spaceship, a saucer, trails us. Oval windows line an upper bulge. An alien with an evil grin looms at the helm. The alien has tentacles instead of arms.

A laser strikes our ship. The metal sizzles.

The corgi pulls us up and out of the dust. He brings us to bear on the enemy ship. I have the weapons controls in my hands, a yoke with round buttons on the handles. I return fire. Green bolts to the alien's red. The shots find their mark but glance off.

At the last moment, the corgi pulls us from the collision course. We streak into empty sky. G-forces squeeze me. I think we're safe, but the red lasers train in on us again. One strikes the ship like an ax striking wood. Warning lights twinkle on the control console. An alarm sounds. Aroooga. Aroooga.

The corgi directs us to a rogue planet, floating alone through space. No sun to warm it. No moons to keep it company. We come in too fast. We slam into the planet's craggy surface, skidding to a stop. Behind us, a rooster tail of orange dust.

The corgi puts on his space helmet, so I put on mine. It's a perfect glass globe. I hope it's a substance stronger than glass. He pops open the cockpit, and we climb out and inspect the damage. I'm no spaceship engineer, but I'd say we're fucked.

"This doesn't look good," says the corgi through the spacesuit's intercom. KJ's voice is distorted by static.

I scan the sky, but there's no sign of the enemy ship.

"How will we get home?" I ask.

The corgi walks toward the horizon. There's horizon in all directions. I follow. The ground crunches beneath my boots. The nascent star system rises ahead, a blurry moon.

The corgi points at the system. His spacesuit has fingers even though he doesn't.

"I'm comforted," he says, "that dust seeks out order. It wants form." He points into the void beyond the star system. "I'm comforted that everything is dust depending on how far away you are when you view it." KJ's voice is clearer now. The corgi turns to me. "Is it okay that I'm okay with being an insignificant speck in the universe? The idea of meaning is such a burden. Isn't it easier to mean nothing?"

I'm not used to the corgi asking me questions. Usually, the conversation flows the other way. I don't answer.

"If I don't mean anything," says the corgi, "then it's no big deal when I'm gone."

On a rogue planet at the universe's very center, I should have a profound reply. Giant leaps for humankind and whatnot. The numbness from my fingers claims my tongue.

"Find it," says the corgi.

The window AC unit shuts off. My apartment is as silent as space. The corgi is back on the sheet of paper. No spacesuit. No spaceship. No new planets to explore.

Pain. Nothing but pain. I lie down. My body is too heavy. G-forces pin me to the bed.

July 3
...

I sit on the floor, leaning against the couch, playing *Final Fantasy X*. I've beaten the game four times before. There are no surprises left in the storyline. But I like the repetitive act of leveling up my characters. Fighting monster after monster. By the end of the game, my characters will be so powerful it's hardly worth facing the final boss. He doesn't stand a chance.

I can't play for too long, though. Tension creeps up from my shoulders into my neck and nests in the spot behind my eye. I save the game and turn off the console and stare at the black screen of my TV. If the phosphenes came now, I'd see a star-filled sky.

A knock on my door, which is strange because you can't enter the building without being buzzed in. I look through the peephole. Have I ever used the peephole before? I always know who'll be there before they knock.

Hildie's face and Ollie over her shoulder. Their features are fish-eyed. I debate on whether I should let them in. I remember that I gave Hildie and Dolores—and KJ—the code for the building's front door. I glance back at the clock. It's still evening. It's been evening for weeks.

This seems like a dumb decision to be giving so much thought to, so I open the door.

Hildie and Ollie walk in. Hildie, I get, but Hildie-plus-one, I'm not sure how I feel about that. My bed is unmade. In the tiny kitchenette, a tower of dishes threatens to topple out of the sink. The game controller remains where I left it on the floor. At least there's no dirty underwear lying around. My pride swells that I haven't sunk that low. Yet.

Hildie taps the controller with the toe of her paint-spattered, purple Chuck.

"*Final Fantasy?*" she asks.

"Ten," I say.

I only have a few games and play them over and over.

"No time to save Spira now," she says. "We're going out."

Ollie doesn't speak. His eyes brim with ghosts.

I want to go out. I really do. I'm endlessly bored. I miss seeing people. But I'm also terrified. If not terrified, then conditioned. I believe that any activity can cause a migraine. Any action I take more than sitting fixed leads to pain.

The inside of my head is a hot stovetop I've learned not to touch.

"Sure," I say.

"I invited Dolores, too, but I don't know if she'll come."

Hildie is distant in this moment, a star so far away it's hard to believe we're part of the same constellation. She's been able to move forward while Dolores and I are stuck in place.

I put on shoes. I check my hair in the mirror. Miraculously, I look alright. I'm bathing and all that. I'm still vain.

The heat outside is a physical object. A popcorn thunderstorm passed through this afternoon, bursting out of nowhere for five minutes, leaving as quick as it came. It's made the air wet and dense.

There are more people out than I expected. Tomorrow is a holiday, I remember. I remember, too, that the day after that is Hildie's birthday. She was born on the fifth because on the fourth someone set off a firework near her mom, triggering early labor.

I'll be expected to be back out again tomorrow evening.

"How's the show coming?" I ask her.

"Getting close," she says. "I've got three paintings going at once, which isn't how I usually work. Makes me feel like I'm on an assembly line."

We enter Pinkie's and nothing's changed. Time can't touch the place because it was old from the day it opened. People sit at the bar in the same seats where their grandparents sat. A black and white photograph superimposes the scene. Time and space are bullshit.

Hildie's buying, so I choose whiskey from the well. I accept charity but only cheaply. She and Ollie order beers. The bar is full but one of the booths is free, so we take it. The walls over the booth are covered with photos of semi-famous people who've come here for drinks. An infamously racist local politician is framed above Hildie's head. Someone has scratched "fuck you" into the acrylic over his face. That someone was Hildie.

I can't tell if Hildie and Ollie are formally dating. Since I've known her, Hildie has had two partners, one woman and one man, both of whom were more her type than Ollie here. I'll have to ask her the next time he's not around.

A person appears at the end of the table. She's backlit, a shadow angel haloed by a Pabst-branded lamp.

"So, you're alive," she says.

I look to my companions at the table, but this person is speaking to me. She shifts out of the backlight. I decode her face. Kat. I haven't seen her since our first date. Our only date. I've hardly thought about her.

"Have a seat," says Hildie.

She gestures for me to scoot over and make room.

Kat sits and presses right up against me. She's a wobbly mess.

I'm back in a quadrilateral constellation. But this one feels off. Only Hildie and I are supposed to be a part of the shape. The other two are rogues, drifting through.

"I'm Hildie," says Hildie.

"Kat," says Kat.

If it's possible to slur a three-letter word, Kat does it.

Hildie waves for Matt's attention at the bar, and then she points at me and holds up two fingers. *Another for him and make it a double.* Matt pours the double and brings it over.

Hildie's message is clear. She wouldn't want me to fool around with drunk Kat unless I, too, was drunk. I'm not particularly in the mood. I don't remember what mood I'm supposed to be in.

Either Ollie doesn't talk much, or he doesn't talk much around me. His shirt is too small, or exactly the right size to look too small over his muscles. When did Hildie start liking musclemen?

Kat talks as if I know a single thing about her. She tells stories about people I've never met. She fails to provide context.

I try to engage Hildie in conversation, the one person who's speaking and making any sense, but she's starting to get physical with Ollie. When they leave, I'm not surprised.

When I stand up to leave, Kat latches onto my arm. I think I'll say goodnight and wait with her while she calls for a ride. But she kisses me. I'm surprised to find her tongue in my mouth. We end up outside my building. She drags me to the front door.

At this point, I go along with it. I don't mean to say I'm not interested. There's some relief to know that my baser impulses can still win out.

Halfway through the act, a migraine aura sets in. My sense of scale goes haywire. Limbs extend and motions distort. Our bodies present new, more interesting shapes. Kat is far, far away, but we're connected. I'm okay with all of this. I'm getting into it. Before the pain, a migraine might be a party drug.

The headache starts as soon as we finish. I totter to the bathroom and clean up and take a pill. Kat's passed out when I come back to bed. I snug her up in the blanket and lie face-up.

I spend hours awake with the hurt. The AC unit runs and I'm tunneling through space. I fall into a shitty sleep and later into a real sleep. My eyes crack open to daylight. Kat is up and naked and hungover. I help her locate her clothes. They're impressively scattered.

I brush my teeth. She borrows toothpaste and scrubs her teeth with a paper towel.

We walk to the breakfast place next door and eat greasy food to settle our stomachs. We don't talk but for pleasantries. What would I say to her? My head aches dully.

After breakfast, we hug goodbye. So ends our second date.

July 3, again

The triptans didn't work last night. The pain was incessant. The throb persisted and evolved. When I fell asleep it was there. I dreamed of accidents and injuries.

In the articles I read about migraines—and that's mainly all I read anymore—there's always talk of placebos, and how drugs that perform better than placebo become the ones doctors prescribe. But the articles gloss over the success of the placebos themselves. Just the suggestion of getting better is enough to feel that way. Temporarily, at least.

The triptans worked the first few times. I would take a dose and in a couple hours the pain would relent. Now that the expectations of relief have become less profound, the effects of the drug have, too. A couple hours turns into four, into six, into eight. Relief from pain turns into less pain turns into nothing at all.

I wonder if my doctor could prescribe sugar pills. Different shapes and colors. Refer me to a shrink or for a massage. The cure isn't in the treatments, anyway, but in the attention given by someone who claims to be able to help. I want the attention. I want someone to care about the hurt.

I don't know what I feel about Kat. I don't know if I'm supposed to feel anything.

My brain's in a better spot this morning. It's cliché to feel better the morning after, isn't it? The hormones have chased away the heaviness I always wake up with, anymore. I'm practically buoyant.

I enter the coffee shop and KJ's empty stool doesn't wreck me. This is the first time I've seen it and not felt as if it's been picked up and smashed across my back.

No, I don't know if I like Kat, but I like the attention she pays to me.

Tomorrow, this feeling will fade.

I try not to think about tomorrow.

July 4
...

Dolores, Hildie, and Ollie plan to meet at my apartment. Ollie arrives first. We spend a few awkward minutes sitting side-by-side on the couch, not talking. I think to play *Super Smash Brothers*. He's not particularly good, but I go easy on him. I buzz Dolores and Hildie in. When they come up, Ollie and I are laughing.

Dusk is already settling. We trek down to the east end of the river and spread a blanket on a hill. River Street glows and hums to our left. Lights shine up the bridge's cables. The fireworks will launch from Hutchinson Island in the river's middle.

Kids dart around with sparklers. Rapid stars.

There's an old photo of me on this hill, maybe sitting on this same blanket. I'm mid-conversation with my ex-girlfriend, Jill, though at the time we weren't yet a formal couple. The photo documents a life that should have happened, I think. But Jill moved away and became an ex and there've been other exes since then. KJ's head sneaks into the corner of the photo. The camera flash caught his eyes, turning them red, full of lasers.

Blake told me Jill moved back to town.

A firework whistle-hisses into the sky. Hildie jumps up. Every year when we come out for the fireworks, I mainly watch her instead of the show. The way she loves this is a special kind of purity. She reminds me that the end of childhood is a choice. We can choose to go back, once in a while.

This close, you feel the explosions as much as hear them, a thump in your chest and heat on your skin.

Ollie is by Hildie's side. He blocks my view of her, so I watch him instead. The ghosts in his eyes are frightened away by the fireworks. Or he sees the same purity in Hildie that I see, and the ghosts can't stand that.

The fireworks finale is constant light and rumble. Filaments of smoke drift east, off toward the ocean. The singed stench of gunpowder chokes the air. The booms echo. The crowd all along River Street claps and hollers.

I wonder if they're applauding the fireworks or the people who launched them.

Hildie sort of hops in place. She's so excited. She's able to contain such excitement.

Somebody's playing patriotic country songs on a portable speaker.

Dolores scoots over and leans against me. She smooths the blanket where she'd been sitting.

The crowds scan the empty sky. The show's over, but they're scared to miss an encore.

Hildie acquires a sparkler from somewhere. She runs in loops with the kids. Ollie has a sparkler, too. He's not quite as carefree, but he's getting there.

"Today was a good day," I say.

"Was it?" asks Dolores.

"Better, at least."

"Time and wounds, huh?"

"Time is bullshit," I say.

She mimics the sound of a laugh. It's not exactly laughing.

"I like that," she says.

Flashes of fireworks appear in front of my eyes, but they fade. Nothing else happens.

Today was a good day.

July 7
...

Pain researcher Fernando Cervero points out that pain isn't a single event but three in sequence. There's the physical reaction to an injury, followed by an emotional reaction, and finally a cognitive response. Hurt leads to fear or anger leads to a decision.

The end of pain is always *thinking* about the pain. The end of pain is awareness.

Inasmuch as pain ever *ends*.

July 8

...

I'm trying defiance.

Yesterday's migraine lingers this morning. The detonations in my brain are gone, but the smoke remains.

I'm the first to arrive at Breakfast Club. If my body is going to betray me, I'm going to ignore it. I'm going to spite it. I'm going to punish it for punishing me.

It's just me and the local weirdos up this early. One middle-aged guy, Marty, sits on a sofa, sipping coffee and reading a book on psychology. He's been reading psychology books for the decade I've known him. He has a Hitler/Chaplin mustache. If you're not careful, he'll share his vast learning with you. He'll corner kids from the art school to impart his wisdom. He has an excess of ideas on human sexuality.

After the fireworks I thought I'd found what the corgi was asking me to find. But a single good day fades. You need slightly more good days than bad for the good to count. Everything is ratios.

What would Marty's books have to say about that?

Out the window a BMW glides into the no-parking zone at the corner. A besuited man steps out and enters the coffee shop. His watch gleams gold, and his sunglasses bear the logo of a luxury brand. He removes the sunglasses and places them in the suit's breast pocket.

There are so many fucking law offices in downtown Savannah.

Hildie shows up, and then Dolores. Ollie comes in last, and I'm happy to see him. We have the beginnings of a bond. He fills in boxes on today's crossword puzzle. There are warring pulls from Ollie on one side and KJ's empty stool on the other. I've been missing having a friend of a certain sort.

Not everything that feels like betrayal is betrayal.

Maybe this will be another good day. Maybe I can get the math right.

I drink a second refill. My blood is coffee. My blood is an antidepressant.

Somebody sets a purse on KJ's stool. I can't be pissed about it. Not like we're saving the seat for anyone. Not like I could tell them we have a friend on the way.

Hildie smiles and says *hi* to the person. The person hugs me from behind.

Holy shit, it's Kat.

"Hey," I say.

Kat goes back to the stool. Why is she here? How did she know that I'd be here? I was drunk, our night together a blur, but I'd never have invited her to Breakfast Club. Ollie's presence here is still barely tolerable.

Did Kat come downtown specifically for this? Does she work downtown? Has she lived next door to me this whole time?

I squeeze Dolores's knee. She nods that it's okay. It's okay that this strange person is sitting in a seat that doesn't belong to her. It's okay that so many new shapes are forming within our constellation.

Dolores introduces herself. Dolores is a saint. I've forgotten how kind Dolores can be, how her face can beam goodness, how she can summon a warm halo over whoever she wants to welcome. I'm glad her kindness has survived. I remember why we're friends and why I value the friendship so much.

When a loss is big enough, you assume other things were lost alongside it.

Kat pulls out a laptop. I can't see what she's working on. I don't know what she does in her spare time. I don't know what she does in her regular time.

Hildie slides over her sketchbook. In the corner of the page, she's written a note: "I hope you don't mind."

I mind like a motherfucker.

"Sure," I say.

Why did Hildie invite this person, this stranger, to the most sacred place we share?

Chris takes Kat's order. She orders a drink where the ratio of coffee to sugar is skewed toward the latter. When Chris asks what size, she says *grande*.

Dolores leans in. "You look a little panicked, bro."

I force myself to write. I accumulate a collection of gibberish. Chris brings Kat's drink to her in a ceramic mug. She seems confused about how to operate it.

"Don't ruin a thing before it starts," Dolores whispers to me.

I want to tell her that sometimes a thing is ruined when you find it. But that's the kind of thought someone who ruins things before they start would think.

Besides the bookends of Kat and Ollie, this is an almost normal morning. The caffeine has relieved the lingering pain in my head. Tension tautens my neck, but I'm getting used to that. Dolores is writing. Hildie sketches. Marty is over there talking about sexuality to two art school kids.

A loud, popping crunch draws everyone's attention outside. One of those massive tour buses, like the kind rock stars use, is trying to turn onto the square, sideswiping the illegally parked BMW. I feel the grinding noise in my teeth. The BMW's bumper shears clean off. The besuited man leaps up and runs outside and waves his arms in a *no, no, no* gesture. He screams at the bus's tinted windows. The bus pulls forward, eating into the BMW's side panel. *No, no, no.*

I say "oh shit," but I'm laughing and Hildie's laughing and Dolores joins in, too. This would be a moment KJ loved. He'd have guffawed. He had a laugh like an animal in distress.

The bus tries to reverse, but that fucks up matters worse. It's impossible to know where the BMW ends and the bus begins. Their surfaces have fused.

A cop shows up. Blue lights bounce off the coffee shop's walls. The siren bleeps, a greeting.

Ollie has joined us watching but doesn't derive the same mirth from the situation. He's the sort of person who might aspire to a BMW. Kat doesn't get the joke, either. But how can I explain it? It's a joke built on other jokes. The three of us—me, Dolores, and Hildie—have been setting up the punchline for years.

I slug back the rest of my coffee. It's time for work. I rub my eyes. The strobing light shows inside the lids.

I pack up my stuff. Kat packs up her stuff, too. I say bye to everyone. Kat says bye to everyone, too. I walk toward the door, and Kat follows.

Before I leave, though, I stop by Marty and ask him, "What do you know about grief?"

This extracts him from the art school kids. My small act of heroism for the day. He exits with me and Kat.

The BMW guy is yelling at the cop and then the bus driver and then the cop again.

Marty cradles his massive textbook. He explains about grief, but I'm not listening. I could teach a class on the subject, myself.

We pass the jampacked antique shop. In the center window there are three portraits of dead Victorian kids with locks of their real hair pasted above the faces like bad toupees.

At the corner, Marty peels off. He lives in the building next to mine. He never strays farther than a few blocks from home.

Kat's still here. I wonder if she intends to follow me to the TV station. I have a dark office with a locking door, but I dismiss that thought. I relish it because such thoughts have been absent for so long.

I note all the BMWs that drive by. There are more than you'd think. So many law offices downtown.

In Madison Square we pass the bronze statue of Sergeant Jasper, lofting a flag with one hand and stanching his mortal wound with the other. All around the poor dying guy, people sit on benches in the dappled shade, drinking coffees and reading papers.

Kat stops, and I realize we're at her car. Was she following me, or was I following her, or were we both assuming we were being followed by the other?

She leans in, and I opt for a hug. I think she hoped for kissing. Save that for our next date. I realize we'll probably go out again.

She swipes the hair from her face and coyly pouts. She's better at this game than I am. She probably doesn't consider it a game. I wait while she drives away and feel relieved when she's gone.

An acute pounding behind my eye. It fades. I stand motionless, a monument, hoping the hurt won't return.

My Personal History of Pain
Part V
...

We were at a tourist bar on River Street, a place we only came whenever Dolores and I got the itch to play ping pong. I was on a hot streak, toppling Hildie then Dolores then Blake and up now against KJ, which would be a win most definitely, his skills in any sport comparable to a toddler, ping pong maybe worst of all. He could miss even the most obvious arcing eephus lobbed his way. Usually, his swings missed outright. The shots he did connect with rebounded from his paddle in scattered directions that statistically should have found the table more often than they did. He was so bad at sports he broke math.

Anyway, we were playing, me serving gimmes, him floundering, zero rallies, just picking the ball up from the floor time and again. I should mention we were getting drunk, and I was getting annoyed, so on one of KJ's rare returns, I smashed it back as hard as I could and scored a point that was so far beyond his skill level I think it embarrassed him.

"Nice grunt," he said.

He readied himself for my next serve, crouching low, holding the paddle in front of his face, edge to the table, an eye peeking around either side. His gaze locked on me, face a scowl. This was his retaliation, mocking me for taking a silly game too seriously. But I was still irritated, so instead of getting the point and laughing, I launched a quick serve. KJ reared back, cocked his arm, and unleashed a mighty swing at the ball, whiffing entirely. His paddle slipped free from his grip, skipped on his side of the table, spinning end over end, over the net, and the butt of the handle impacted directly on my hip bone.

I yelped.

Dolores, Hildie, and Blake all laughed.

The bartender yelled over at us, "Take it easy."

KJ tipped an imaginary hat at the bartender.

"That's gonna bruise," KJ said to me.

That's how he liked to apologize, by acknowledging the damage.

I rubbed my hip. "I still won the point, and now you don't have a paddle."

"Don't need one," he declared.

We finished the game, me with a paddle in each hand, KJ slapping at the ball with his open palm. He commentated our play in a faux-announcer voice, rollercoastering the pitch and diction. By the end we were in hysterics, score long forgotten, random bar patrons watching and cheering on KJ, the clear favorite. Finally, one of KJ's slaps landed. I reached for the ball with the paddle in my off hand but couldn't connect. The onlookers erupted in cheers. He thrust his arms high in victory, declaring himself the champion. One point enough. And who was I to argue?

Dolores jumped up to hug him. Hildie and Blake dumped a box of extra ping pong balls over his head. We drank and celebrated with strangers. The evening blurred.

I limped home at the end of the night, my hip stiffening. In the morning, the bruise would be deep purple, evolving over the week to sickly green. And then one day, without me noting the date or the time or the circumstances, the bruise was gone altogether.

July 21
...

I discover that a rum and Coke can curb a migraine at the start. If there's any science behind this, I don't know. I don't know if it's a placebo effect. I don't know if the caffeine counteracts whatever goes on in the blood vessels of my head. I don't know if the alcohol numbs the trigeminal ganglion or stops my nociceptors from winding up to a hypersensitized state. I don't know if I'm using any of those terms correctly.

Sometimes, though, the drink helps. I can't claim that about much else.

I procure a rum and Coke from Pinkie's to go. It comes in a small plastic cup, a size between shot glass and Solo. That the City of Savannah lets you carry a drink around outside remains a miracle.

It's late but daylit. Summer afternoons in Savannah run on repeat.

I sweat my way to Touchdown Video. Touchdown hasn't rented out videos in a decade, except for the porn section in back. Up front is all comic books and trading cards. Beige curtains drape the doorway between sections.

The comics are displayed on rickety metal racks, Frankenstein assemblages of modular closet parts. Every tile of the drop ceiling is water stained and sagging. A moldering smell chokes the air. I convince myself it's the rotting tiles, not wafting from the porn room.

KJ and I came here every Wednesday after work. New comic book day.

It's my first time visiting in months. The owner hulks behind the counter. His black t-shirt has faded to gray. The neckline droops across his shoulders, an ashen lei, no elastic left.

"Where you been?" he asks.

I tactfully tell him that KJ died.

"I figured something like that," he says.

I tell him about the migraines.

"I had a cashier who had those once," he says. "Fuckin' bullshit is what it is. He'd call in sick and I'd be like what's wrong and he'd say headache, like that's a goddamn excuse to miss work. Hell, I've had a headache since 1993."

"What happened in '93?" I ask.

"I opened *this* place."

He answers the phone and is extra rude to whoever's on the other end. His anger makes me anxious.

The AC flutters the curtains dividing the comics from the porn. A siren's call for some, I suppose.

I browse the racks of new issues. On the covers all the heroes, all the villains, even the bystanders have pained expressions.

The porn room curtains part, and Marty comes out. As far as I've observed, his only two activities are reading psychology and watching porn on VHS. I avoid eye contact as Marty checks out.

The owner's still on the phone. He rents out porn with the who-gives-a-damn of a grocer selling grapes. Marty leaves. The ancient brass bell over the door sounds more like a death rattle than a ding. KJ would stare straight at anyone who had porn in hand. An accusation or a judgment. You've never seen so many grown men blush.

I thumb through issues of comics, looking for a book to KJ's taste. He went for the weird stuff. Indies and fringe. Superheroes, too, of course. Nobody loved Metamorpho, The Element Man, as much as KJ.

The world quivers. Phosphenes sparkle.

All the flat, pained faces from the comics swarm wherever I look. A 360-degree collage of superheroes. An epic crossover event. The drawings shift and swirl. I spy KJ's corgi in the crowd.

I slug back the rest of my rum and Coke.

The auras have a progression. Glitchy electrical impulses spreading over my brain. I can see the mechanisms inside my skull in the sequence of visions.

The owner slams down the phone's receiver. The crack reverberates. He points at my cup.

"No drinks, man."

I rattle the ice. "It's empty."

"Sounds like somethin' in there to me."

I've got a comic in my hand. I picked it up at random. It flops limply. I can't angle it cover-side-up to read the title.

The room segments into blocks framed by white spaces, the gutters between comics panels.

I take the comic to the counter and pay in cash.

Outside, the city is guttered and getting worse. Existence in shards. My life inside a kaleidoscope.

I stumble into a bike rack, shin-first. I shout a string of profanities. My words appear around me in speech bubbles.

Pedestrians gawk at me and my empty cup and make wrong assumptions.

I hurry back to Pinkie's for a refill. Enough time has passed that it's dark. Time and space are bullshit.

I stand outside on the sidewalk. The concrete is the hardest substance in the universe.

The stars come out. Small enough to see through my fractured vision. The constellations, though, are scattered all to hell. A sailor would be hopelessly lost on a night like this.

I think of heroes. Heroes save us when we're lost.

Save me, Metamorpho.

I finish the second rum and Coke. The world reassembles. Maybe *I'm* the hero for putting it back together again. Maybe this pain is the price I pay for my powers.

I get a third drink to go, but the only place I go is home.

July 22

Another victim of migraines: the guy who invented the kaleidoscope. I imagine he made it to show what an aura looks like.

To share his shattered world.

July 24
...

I want to know what pain *means*.
But it doesn't mean shit.

August 1

...

I want the doctor to tell me what's wrong. No, that's not quite right. I can already list all that's wrong with me. Even without pain, life is simply ticking off items on that list.

Instead, I want the doctor to tell me what's causing the wrongness. I want a tangible diagnosis, an x-ray to point to and say, *this*.

The word *migraine* denotes symptoms, a list of wrongnesses. But it never addresses the cause. *Migraine* doesn't tell me how to stop feeling so tired. A burning need for sleep. Hoping the endless worry will finally end. I'm so tired of my head threatening to descend again into pain.

Might not looming pain be a form of pain itself?

So, I'm back at the doctor. I banter with another old man in the lobby. This one survived a heart attack. He's proud of that fact. If I asked him to, he'd unbutton his shirt and show me the scars on his chest.

The nurse calls my name. I go back into the guts of the office. I swear the rooms have been rearranged. Like one of those pocket-sized plastic puzzles where you slide tiles around to arrange a picture. For those puzzles to work, the key is that one square stays empty.

I've lost weight, according to the scale. My blood pressure is good. My heart rate, too. My temperature is within a normal range for a human.

I sit for lifetimes on the paper-topped examination table. I memorize the posters on the walls. I learn all the parts of the sinuses. I calculate my optimum heart rate for aerobic exercise.

When was the last time I went for a run?

I guess at the number of swabs in the glass jar on the counter.

The doctor comes in, and I don't know why I'm here. I've been on this same table in this same room in the same office in this same pain. Deja goddamn vu. I repeat phrases the doctor endures daily.

Time is bullshit. I'm glad it's bullshit for someone else and not just me. Poor doctor.

She's bored by me. I'm a glitch in her day. I'm a person who can't be helped, her eyes say. Ghosts flit there. I wonder if she's haunted by patients she's lost. I wonder if she considers me a haunting.

I tell her about the rum and Cokes. She thinks on that for a moment. She tells me *moderation*. Too much rum could backfire.

I tell her the triptans aren't doing it for me anymore.

I only take them because they tend to make KJ's corgi come to life, but I don't tell the doctor that.

There's nothing more she can do, she says. She gives me a referral to a neurologist. The ghost that is me recedes in her eyes. Referral as exorcism. I'm relieved that she's relieved to be done with me.

The fluorescent lights cause the world to pulse.

I pay at the front desk and step outside into sunlight. The heat has mass. In August in Savannah the streets sweat.

I don't for a second contemplate going to work. I almost wish my boss were harder on me. But I skip hours and I skip days and as long as the job gets done, she doesn't notice my physical self. Another form of fading.

I walk toward home. The buildings and houses melt. The tops drip down like ice cream. Shingles and bricks and glass mingle into mud.

I call the neurologist while I walk. The receptionist says they can see me in November. Three months away.

How badly would my brain have to be broken for an earlier appointment?

I sit on a bench at a bus stop, but the slats are too hot. I get up and find a bench in a shady spot in the square. The shade is minimal. I melt alongside the city. We're all one puddle.

It's miserable. Not the headache, though one's on the way. This heat oppresses. It won't relent. Not until deep within fall. I schedule an appointment with cooler weather.

I wait and I wait and I wait. I've lost hope that I'll ever arrive at whatever it is I'm waiting for.

August 8
...

Dolores sends me a text. I reply, *Sorry, migraine.*
Hildie calls. I tell her, *Sorry, migraine.*
Blake's down at Pinkie's. *Sorry, migraine.*
It's a perfect summer day outside. Birds chirp directly at me. *Sorry, migraine.*
The corgi stirs on his page. *Sorry, buddy, migraine.*

August 14
...

Kat's been coming to my place some evenings. We don't have a schedule. She'll text in advance. I'll say *sure come on over* and scramble for twenty minutes to straighten up. I'm always washing dishes when she gets here.

We watch TV or a movie. We don't talk much. She doesn't like *Naruto*.

Today, between her text and her arrival, my vision glitches. I'm washing dishes, as usual. There's a saucer in the sink under the faucet. Water sheets off the sides, a perfect circle. I think of the fountain in Forsyth Park. I think of all the tourists posing for photos in front of it.

My sink is the most photographed kitchen fixture in the city.

The starbursts of phosphenes appear as part of the water. Whitecaps on waves.

I pick up the saucer, but it slips free. My fingertips are numb. The saucer cracks into four wedges. It's a cheap piece of shit, so I'm not upset. There's a weird orange stain on it that no washing could remove. The stain survives the break.

Water strikes the metal of the sink, pinging.

Kat knocks on the door. I yell for her to come in, but she doesn't, so I go to the door and open it. She kisses me, heavy and wet. There's booze on her breath. Her shorts fall off, and she's stepping out of them. I haven't closed the door yet. The sink's still on.

The sex is a battle between my body and my head. I give up trying and let Kat take over. She doesn't seem to mind. She doesn't seem to notice. I don't need to be here, but of course I do. She finishes, and I don't. I can't feel how I'm supposed to. I prop up on the bed at the angle that hurts the least.

So much of what I do now I do out of obligation.

Kat goes to the bathroom. She comes out and raids my liquor stash. She shuts off the sink. She mixes cheap vodka with whatever's in my fridge. I ask for a rum and Coke.

She shimmies up the bed with the drinks. I accept mine and chug it all down. I think I might hurl but choke back the feeling. Kat's still naked. I marvel at her skin. A shoulder here, a stomach there.

"Headache?" she asks.

I nod. Nodding is a mistake. I depress my head deeper into the pillow. I immobilize myself.

Kat leans back and inspects me. I recognize this look. I'm a skeptic myself.

"Maybe it's all in your head," she says.

"Well," I say, "it's a *head*ache."

"You know what I mean."

She drinks her drink. Her eyes turn inward. She watches the alcohol mix with her blood.

Kat's trying to help, I get that, but she's not a natural caretaker. She's young and having fun and wants to remain free of this responsibility. This burden.

"Could it be stress?" she asks.

I've considered stress and grief and depression. I've read enough to know those conditions can be comorbid. I've come to adore the word *comorbid*. So many things can be parts of other things.

Kat suggests more possible causes. I've considered every possibility before. Advice is a form of echo.

Giving advice is an admission, too. My pain makes people uncomfortable. I'm a reminder of human physicality. I'm a reminder of the ways the body can break. Because you can't think *thank god not me* without also thinking *oh god what if* that *was* me.

"Why don't we go out for another drink and see if that helps?" she says.

She rises and lights the overhead to find her clothes. When did it get dark?

I try to move to a sitting position. The pain flares, engulfing my whole head. I settle back into the pillow. My breaths are quick gasps.

Kat fastens her bra in a fraction of the time it took me to unhook it. She eyes me. No pity, no concern. Just disgust. She pulls on her shirt. Her face reappears through the neck hole.

"Don't think so tonight," I say.

She's figured this out already. I speak to fill the gap.

"This sucks, you know?" she says.

I do.

She un-musses her hair. The sight of her. My heart beats faster. That's all it takes for pain. I remember why I first approached her at Pinkie's. A few months ago, we might have been a couple. Now, her expression says I've entered the role of villain.

"Look," she says, "I'm going out. If you feel better," she points at her temple, "you should give me a call."

She leaves. She takes her shitty vodka drink with her in one of my nice glasses.

Can you miss someone and not miss them at the same time? Can you feel that way seconds after they leave?

I may be a villain in her story, but she's antagonized me from the start. I won't call her tonight. She wasn't talking about tonight, anyway.

August 16
...

I've talked about pain as if it's a small machine I could pluck out with a pair of tweezers. It's not a thing itself, though, but a signifier of other things.

Try plucking the green from grass.

I look out the window at the trees and the traffic and a limping panhandler. I imagine stealing the world's colors. I wander a grayscale city. The panhandler holds out a paper cup for an indigo, a fuchsia, a jade. Any color at all.

The pain is not its cause, and the cause is not the pain. It's probably wrong to think of the cause as singular. If I looked back through these diaries, I could locate several possible triggers in each entry. What's the point in listing triggers if the list never limits, only grows?

Everyone in pain, everyone ill, everyone hurting hopes for a reason. Because if we can understand it, then we can beat it.

The world is fuller of hurt than relief.

The sky *looks* blue more than the sky *is* blue.

Pain turns you into a half-assed philosopher.

Today, clouds decolor everything.

I can see the top of a container ship steaming into port. I read the names of foreign companies on the containers. So many languages I don't speak. With so many words from so many different places, I have no idea where the ship might be coming from. It's simultaneously sailed from every other port in the world and only coalesces into a single ship at its destination.

The logo on a dented gray container is a four-pointed star.

I watch it glide by. I watch the panhandler. I watch whatever draws my eye. None of it makes more sense than the rest.

Everything blends to beige.

Everything merges into the hurt.

August 29

...

Every year, Blake throws a party in Forsyth Park over Labor Day weekend. I'm up with him early, balancing on a rickety ladder, threading a hose and extension cord from his condo through the oaks arching over Whitaker Street. The branches form a green wormhole. Sunlight pulses through gaps in the leaves.

Cars slow as they pass beneath us. I want to tell the drivers that the slower they go, the more likely it is we'll drop something on them. Move along. Keep on truckin'.

We finish and stow the ladder. In the park proper, we unroll four Slip 'n Slides, arranged in a plus sign, and inflate a jumbo kiddie pool at the intersection. Other folks drop off grills, a total of five. Eight coolers. Charcoal and beers. A giant speaker blares summer-friendly pop.

Blake and I take turns rinsing off with the hose. The water runs hot. In August in Savannah people are sweat monsters. Blake doffs his t-shirt and wrings it out. I marvel at his skin. A shoulder, a stomach.

He crosses over to his condo to change into a swimsuit. I stay with the stuff and wait.

A game of pick-up football is in progress across the park. From far away it looks like random sprinting back and forth. No purpose. Dolores and I used to join in the Saturday morning games. I'm a passable wide receiver. KJ joined sometimes, too. He was always the last to be picked for a team. He was so bad at sports.

Dolores arrives. She lugs a cooler full-up with various meats. She fires a grill. The charcoal catches and belches smoke.

Blake returns and then more people come and it's a party. Lines form at all the Slip 'n Slides. People fill the kiddie pool to bursting, barely room for water. A haze of grill smoke grays the air.

People at a party eddy and swirl. Shifting constellations. It's impossible to predict who'll end up where.

A cop car cruises past at half-hour intervals.

Everyone's half-naked and happy. So many old friends I haven't seen since KJ's memorial.

Hildie splashes in the pool. She claims the hose and turns it on bystanders. Lyn and Pru and Chuck argue over the best technique to use on the Slip 'n Slide so as to not spill their beers.

This is the first summer we haven't all gone together to the beach. I've forgotten the texture of sand. I wonder if we'll ever go to the beach again.

Ollie's standing with me near the grills. He's shirtless. He showcases the kind of muscles it takes self-punishment to sculpt. I don't remove my own shirt because I'm embarrassed at how slack my muscles have become.

Dolores brings me a burger, a little overdone, but that's how I want it because I have an irrational fear of food poisoning at cookouts.

Kat's here, but she faces any direction but mine. The petty part of me wants to chat up someone else to make her jealous. My lazier parts don't make the effort.

I admire Ollie's comfort with silence.

If not lazy, then I'm expectant. I expect a headache, so why strike up a conversation only to abandon it?

Blake cranks the music. More beer arrives as if summoned, coolers magically refilling themselves.

It's odd to watch a tumult from the side. KJ was always in the middle of things. I realize how much I relied on him to pull me in, too.

A police SUV hops the curb and drives straight into the park. Blue lights strobe in my brain.

"Head's up," I yell.

The party's mostly on the up-and-up. A few people pinch joints. Beer in bottles gets poured into plastic cups to make them legal. Open container laws remain a miracle. Blake drops the volume on the music. Deathly quiet.

The SUV stops next to the grills. Our pal Roland hops out. He's a school cop but works evenings at the TV station, running cameras for newscasts. He's old enough to be retired. He's well outside his jurisdiction.

Roland walks over and selects a beer from one of the coolers and pulls the tab. The hiss is the loudest sound in the park. A cheer erupts.

This has suddenly gone from a good party to a great party. People trot over and toast Roland. The music returns. This party is blessed.

Roland joins me and Ollie.

"Should you really drive your truck up in the park like that?" I ask.

"Fuck it," he says, "I'm a cop."

What do the people looking over at us think? I worry that standing with a cop and a soldier is killing my progressive cred. At least the cop is drinking a beer in uniform. At least the soldier is dating an artist. The simplest label is sometimes the wrong one.

Hildie makes rounds with a tray of Jell-O shots. She kisses Ollie and offers the tray. The shots are wiggly jewels in plastic ramekins. Roland grabs one, too. We toast and toss back and swallow.

Another cheer. I hadn't noticed everyone watching again, waiting to see what Roland would do. What a goddamn hero.

Hildie hugs Roland. She barely knows him, but Hildie's that kind of person. She points to the truck.

"Should you be driving after that?" she asks.

Roland pats his ample belly. It stretches the faded black fabric of his uniform. He could be hiding a basketball.

"Let's just say it takes more than two drinks to feel anything."

His radio squawks. It's garbled nonsense to me, but Roland presses a button and replies.

"Gotta go," he says. "Always a call right at the end of my shift."

He places the empty ramekin back on the tray and gives me his beer. The can is down to backwash.

Roland bleats his siren and waves out the window as he drives off. Someone starts singing "Bad Boys" and then everyone at the party joins in. We're actors in a musical. The park is a gigantic stage.

"This is some absolute magical shit," says Ollie.

I look around. I'm a camera panning across a scene in a movie. Ollie's right. These moments, grand and frivolous at once, how many have I missed?

On the other hand, how rare are they?

Eventually, I'm tossing a Frisbee. Later, I end up in the pool. I don't do the Slip 'n Slide. Just the thought of banging my head on the ground triggers a warning in the spot behind my eye. But the pain never comes.

As shocking to feel okay as to hurt.

Then I'm talking to Kat, and even though we don't like each other very much, leaving together is the simplest thing. A method to stretch this moment longer.

August 30
...

This morning after the party I slither out of bed. I instinctively go to the medicine cabinet and grab the giant bottle of ibuprofen. I've used the stuff so often for hangovers that I don't give it a thought until I pop the lid. The rattle of the pills pulls me out of it. I almost drop the bottle.

I return it to the cabinet and back away. The ghost in the mirror is my own face.

Kat snuck out in the night. I text her to check in. I'm glad she's gone but want to make sure she got where she was going.

My mouth tastes like yesterday's booze. I struggle to the kitchen sink for water. I gag on the first sip but force it down.

I put on a pot of coffee. The coffee maker has occupied a shelf in my tiny kitchen for years, but I didn't use it until recently. It was always the coffee shop, instead. Now the forty yards from here to there seem Saharan.

The smell of brewing coffee nauseates me. The burnt pelt of a wild animal. It's some generic blend from the grocery store. The packaging mimics a famous brand.

I turn on the TV and pull up *Naruto*. Three episodes pass before I realize it. I've forgotten to get the coffee. Time is bullshit.

I pour the coffee and take a gulp. It won't go down. I rush to the bathroom and vomit the coffee and all the water I drank plus a boozy liquid I assume is left from the party.

I fetch water again from the kitchen. I sip the coffee.

It's only now I recognize that what I thought was a hangover is really a migraine. The two conditions have intermingled. I missed one for the other. The coarse, cottony feeling in my head homes in on the single spot. Waves of nausea. The light from the TV is rimmed by a rectangle of sunburst. I turn off the TV and I sit there and sit there and sit there.

The morning disappears like that. The afternoon. The evening.

Life is transactional, I guess. A bad day equal trade for a good one.

September Somethingth
...

How do you write about a threat?

Every morning when I wake up, the pain is poised above me. The Hurt of Damocles.

I avoid moving. Once I sit someplace, that's where I tend to stay. An object at rest tends to blah blah blah. I'm always tired.

I drive to work. It isn't any quicker than walking.

Hildie comes by and brings pizza, and we watch *Naruto*.

Dolores comes by and brings sandwiches, and we watch *Naruto*.

Ollie comes by, and we play video games, but I can't play for long before my shoulders tense. Any tension anywhere in my body spreads up my neck and into my head.

I drink rum and Cokes, and then I move to drinking rum neat. Any hint of pain I aim to numb completely. I buy rum by the handle. I try not to notice how quickly the bottles empty.

Today, when Dolores buzzes up, I find her at my front door, crying. Or at least she's recently cried. The skin of her cheeks glistens. Her glasses expand her eyes to frothing oceans. She usually wears contacts.

I give her a dish towel. I don't have tissues. I lead her to the sofa. In the hand without the towel, she clutches an envelope. The paper is lush, a rich cream color. The surface is smudged. The corner of the postage stamp curls up.

I get her a drink, but mainly I'm getting myself one. I split the last of a handle of rum between two glasses. It's okay, I have another handle in the cabinet below.

I trade her the drink for the envelope. Return to sender is scrawled in red under the address. The return address is Dolores's apartment by the park.

The top of the envelope is slit. Who owns a letter opener? Dolores, that's who.

The more I inspect the envelope, the more familiar it becomes.

I pull out the contents. An invitation. To a wedding. One that was supposed to have happened only days ago. Is that right? I don't know the date. I don't know the date today or the date the wedding was supposed to have been. September somethingth.

"I hadn't checked the mail in a few days," says Dolores. "This was sitting on top."

"Shit," I say.

What glitch in post office operations allowed this envelope, sent out months before, to arrive back to Dolores so late? What kind of cosmic taunt is this?

Goddammit, the universe is a cold, uncaring sack of fuck.

There's so much pain in my head. It's growing with my incomprehension. Dolores leans into me and weeps. Heaving sobs. Sobs that could lift large objects.

I'm crying, too, but I'm not sure for the same reasons.

Hildie designed the invitations. The design is playful. The design promises years of mirth within the happy couple's marriage. The design was so right then and is so wrong now.

I try to read the printed date but my vision has blurred.

When the weeping lets up, Dolores asks, "What am I gonna do?"

"There's nothing to be done," I say.

Later, all cried out, she leaves. My own words resound in my head. They're there when I go to sleep, and they linger in the morning. They assume a place alongside the pain, lurking.

I hurt and I doubt and when one ebbs, the other surges.

This is a sort of balance but not a philosophy.

September 15
...

One day with no pain in my head. I don't recognize the sensation when I wake up. The *lack* of a sensation. As increased energy. As optimism. As fresh start.

> An act on the body
>   is only a cure
>   if it happens
> more than once—
> otherwise we call it a miracle.
>
> –Marcelo Hernandez Castillo, "Origin of Theft"

I think, too, that for events we call miracles, we never bothered to look for a second example. Nothing kills a moment as quick as no longer feeling special. Good moments the most mortal of all.

The next day, the hurt returns.

September 28
...

Hildie's art show opens tonight at a gallery on Whitaker Street. My head aches, but I decide to walk there, anyway.

Nothing I choose to do makes the suffering better or worse. Consistency, a small gift.

Daylight is running scarce. The temperature turns forgiving. The restaurants with outdoor seating do good business. Ambient chatter hovers over downtown like a haze.

My breaths are half-sized. My legs fatigue after only a block. I sit for a minute on the stone steps of a building on Liberty Street. A green light bulb buzzes from the pediment. Why green? I've seen the bulb for years but have never given a second thought to the color before.

Mellow Mushroom, a pizza joint, bustles next door. There are so many more restaurants in Savannah now than there used to be, but Mellow is a mainstay. KJ and I used to go there once a week for beer and soft pretzels.

I'm up again and moving.

On Whitaker Street, traffic whizzes by. Whenever I visit a big city, I realize what the word *traffic* really means. In Savannah, it just means a few more cars than I'm used to.

Up ahead, the art gallery occupies a corner storefront, plate glass for exterior walls. It glows yellow, a beacon, guiding suffering ships back to shore. The other shops in the area sit darkened. Clothes and antiques and all sorts of wares reduced to shadows.

Whitaker is one way, and the traffic approaches from behind me. My own shadow starts long on the sidewalk, shortens, and then it's gone until the next car comes.

Is this one shadow reappearing or a series of different shadows?

Is the hurt one pain repeating or many?

I'm only a few minutes after the start time, but the gallery is packed. Since when are artists punctual? Folks love Hildie, though. Through the windows, the well-lit faces of friends, a decade of people I've met in this city. There's almost nobody inside I don't know.

Is there a name for this phenomenon?

It's been months since I frequented the bars where I used to run into my friends.

The double front doors, set in the cropped corner of the building, are propped open. The light dazzles across my skin. I step inside. I wave to Lyn and Pru and Chuck. Hugs and handshakes.

Where the hell you been?

So-and-so said you've been sick?

How you feelin'?

Hildie latches onto my arm. She's wearing a jumpsuit printed with multi-colored dinosaurs.

"Rad jumpsuit," I say.

"Thanks!" she says. "Pain in the ass if you gotta pee, though."

She leads me to Dolores and Ollie. I offer a pair of weak hugs. Hildie is pulled away into other conversations.

People at a party eddy and swirl.

The text Dolores wrote for Hildie is printed on a vinyl sheet clung to the window. The title of the show, which Hildie debated up to the last moment, is *Sufferers*.

The first painting is a reimagining of Joan of Arc. A small label explains it's based on a painting by Jean-Auguste-Dominique Ingres. An eight-by-ten photo of the original hangs by the label. In Hildie's version, Joan's armor has been replaced by a straitjacket, her arms unbound, the straps dangling. On the table where Joan's hidden hand rests, candles and urns have been replaced by amber-colored, white-capped prescription bottles. No halo, but a zigzagging line arching over Joan's head.

I panic. This is the edge of a migraine blind spot. The term is *scotomata*, part of an aura. But it's in the painting itself. My vision is fine. My headache has already started. The visions taper out once the pain begins.

I note the similarity of the words *scotomata* and *stigmata*. I don't know the words' roots.

A caterer with a tray circulates. Dolores, Ollie, and I take flutes of Prosecco.

Further along there's a painting based on Peter Paul Rubens's *Saint Teresa of Ávila's Vision of the Holy Spirit*. The original depicts Teresa on her knees, gazing up into a smudge of light, a blurry Spirit, maybe an angel wing. The light sends out a single shaft with a metal tip. I think it's supposed to be a spear, but it could also be a bullet. In Hildie's version, instead of coming from above, the light emerges from Teresa's own eye. Saint, or movie projector.

Chris greets us. Have I seen him outside of the coffee shop before? Then I remember him at KJ's memorial.

"It's nice," he says, "to see the results of what y'all are working on every morning."

"Only if we ever finish something," I say.

"I like this one," he says, pointing at the painting of Teresa. "It's subtle. Just a couple changes from the original."

"A couple is all it takes," says Dolores.

Chris chuckles and walks on.

This painting starts to bug me. A spear to the eye is too on the nose. But that's not it. Hildie's Teresa is familiar. The face in the painting belongs to Kat.

Did Kat pose for the painting, or on one of those mornings at the coffee shop did Hildie sneak a sketch of her profile.

The risk of having artistic friends is that your life might end up hung on a gallery wall.

A caterer comes by and I exchange my empty flute for an extra full glass of wine. Blake waves from across the room. I check for Kat, but she's not here. I can't tell if I'm glad or sad about that.

The biggest painting doesn't quite fit in. The style is cartoony, though it's based on a Baroque original. The scene is

Abraham about to gut Isaac, right when the angel comes down to end the whole farce. In Hildie's version, the angel is a caricature of KJ. In the upper corner, vacant but for background in the original, there's a comic book speech bubble. Lo the angel speaks, "Don't do it, dude."

That was one of KJ's catchphrases. He'd say it in a pinched, childish voice when one of us was too drunk and about to do something regrettable.

I sense Ollie's stare. He's looking back and forth between me and Dolores. Ghosts in his eyes. A person who knows of hauntings. I wonder if he understands. I wonder if he saw the work in progress and had Hildie explain it to him.

Is there any way to explain a memory to somebody who didn't live it?

Gravity turns heavy. The spot behind my eye writhes. I empathize with Teresa and her spear. I understand wanting to believe in suffering's divine origins.

I gently nudge Dolores to the next painting.

"She told me it would be here," she says, "but I guess you can't be ready for something like that."

There's a quaking under the pain. The old grief. Except grief doesn't get older. It stays young even as it ages you.

We view the next paintings, but they blur. I'm sure they're great. I honestly adore Hildie's work. I'll come back another day and look more closely. I probably won't make the effort.

The final painting. There I am dead center, my naked, scrawny body a god. Instead of a saint having a vision, I'm the vision itself. The original features the stereotypical sexy granddad god, nestled in clouds, surrounded by winged beasts. In Hildie's, I'm among ample pillows, snugged up in an edgeless bed, cats curled around me. There's Hildie II. Instead of a heavenly glow, a table lamp shines on me. The angle of my body has been shifted to allow for my nakedness. Proof I'm no god. Proof of my capacity to suffer.

I lean closer and closer, but I can't focus. I'm suddenly embarrassed by my nudity. I need to cover up.

Blake waves to draw my attention. He points at his own crotch and gives me a thumbs up. Dolores laughs loudly. Blake's washed away the awkwardness. It's just a painting. It's just a dick.

We mingle by the snacks. The air is hazy. Sometimes the suffering is like a foggy bathroom mirror.

I've learned to keep from grimacing when the pain surges. I've learned to fake being okay.

Three new people enter the gallery. I notice because they don't quite fit in. The rest of us are weird artist types. We look the part. Maybe the newcomers are normcore kids, but one of them is too old for that. He's familiar.

Why does everyone look like someone else?

But I know him. Preacherman from the coffee shop. That curly blond hair. He's out of context. I never took him for cultured. He's unartful to the max. The two kids with him hand out religious flyers or pamphlets or some shit like that. So, not arty, after all.

Preacherman makes a round of the paintings. His face scrunches up, either connoisseurship or distaste.

Blake's over and gossiping with us. He's got a new guy with him, but I miss the guy's name. I focus on Preacherman. His presence is an irritation. A mote in the eye. His underlings have failed to hand out their flyers and now loiter near the exit, blankly gawking at the buffed concrete floor.

Preacherman accepts a glass of red wine as he ambles along the gallery walls. He holds the wine with both hands in front of him, a sacrament. He doesn't drink it.

Blake says my name in a sentence and people laugh, so I laugh. Ollie doesn't. He's watching Preacherman, too. Ollie has been professionally trained to detect threats. We both sense danger.

Preacherman stops by the final painting, me in my balls-out glory. He bows his head, mutters a prayer. He lifts his head and slops red wine all over the painting.

Ollie's across the room in one stride. He twists Preacherman's arm and pins it behind his back. The wine glass shatters on the floor. Ollie forces Preacherman to the exit. Red wine drips down my face in the painting. I'd say it looks like blood, but it doesn't.

Hildie sashays over, so casual, and dabs away the wine with cocktail napkins. All's well. The painting could be fresh from her studio. She grins the whole time. She sells it as a part of the show.

The police arrive. Who called them? Certainly not one of Hildie's friends.

Blue lights pulse. We all watch Preacherman get arrested. The windows are a movie screen. Usually, the cops signal the end of a party, but this one's growing rowdy. The caterers are gone and with them the wine. Now it's bottles of bourbon.

All the excitement peaks my blood pressure. The spot behind my eye is about to detonate. I worry I'm dying. *Angor animi.*

I need to go home, but I hate leaving a party early. I move to my painting. Hildie missed one drop of wine. I wish it were on my cheek, a tear, but it drips down my chest.

A punk album cranks from speakers in the ceiling. I can't take it. I slip out into the night.

Heading back along Whitaker, the cars rush right at me. Headlights spear my eyes. The sidewalk vanishes. This suffering has me half out-of-body. I don't remember the rest of the walk except once a car honking when I veered into the street. I'm home without knowing it.

I strip down and climb into bed and imagine being a martyr. But I'm immortal.

No matter how many times the spear strikes, I survive.

October 1

I don't like the word *suffering*.

It's loaded with implications of necessity.

I must suffer this to experience nonsuffering on the other side.

I must endure to reach a state in which endurance is no longer required.

Suffering attaches a carrot to the end of the stick being used to beat you.

Suffering asks you to be grateful because all of this is part of a grand cosmic plan.

No, no, no.

Leave suffering to the saints in Hildie's paintings.

I'll stick with *pain* and *ache* and *hurt*.

October 6

...

At work I have a client edit in the morning. She's a young woman dressed primly, fresh out of a marketing degree at Big State U. Usually, I'm alone in my dark office, mass producing commercial after commercial. Whenever a client comes in, it mucks the process.

This client is cool, though. She slouches the moment she sits down. She cusses a lot in casual conversation. She offers random suggestions for the commercials but mainly lets me do my thing.

She's from a local ad agency, repping a chiropractor. I'm making two variations of the same commercial. One generic and one tagged for holiday gift cards. Odd stocking stuffer, but there you are.

The photog shot us good video, which makes the edit easier. Sparkling white rooms, smiling pseudo-docs, straight-spined customers. There are three chiropractors in all. The mid-thirties one with the gray-flecked goatee does all the talking. He's got the voice for it. He recites his lines from memory and doesn't sound stilted. A gold cross dangles in the open V of his well-starched oxford. Maybe he moonlights as a preacher.

No more pain, the goatee guarantees. I take that for a harmless lie. Harmless, because if you're hurting, then you already know the pain never leaves you.

Lies don't count when they're obvious.

I chat with the agency rep while I edit and mention the migraines. She tells me consultations at the chiropractor are free. The commercial has already repeated this fact over and over and over.

The video of the lobby shows a space made up like a living room. The furniture is the leather kind with rivets at the seams.

An electric fireplace kindles fakely in the corner. A stick of incense burns on the reception desk.

The client breaks for lunch and when she comes back, she brings me coffee and a donut. You'd be shocked how often clients are unaware that I might be hungry. This is our first edit together and she's already my favorite. I might be in love with her a little. Anymore, all it takes is the barest of kindness.

Kat never once showed up with food.

Most of the afternoon the client spends on her phone. It's disorienting to hear her in one ear and the commercial in the other. It triggers a sensation like motion sickness. Some of her calls are professional and some personal.

It's the end of the day when she finally leaves. Tension worms through my shoulders. Termites burrowing in wood. My monitor quavers, an underwater quality. Swaying kelp.

I know what the evening will hold. Pain calls in advance.

I pull up one of the commercials and find the chiropractor's phone number.

It's a big claim, taking away the pain. I'd have settled for far less. I'd have settled for the minimum. But what's the least that can happen now?

My appointment is set for tomorrow morning.

No more pain, claims the chiropractor.

October 7

...

The chiropractor's office is out in Pooler, a suburb of Savannah, a city itself too small to justify suburbs. The town no shit uses the motto "It's cooler in Pooler," which is both lame and a lie.

I-16 is backed up heading into downtown, but I drive against morning traffic. Two straight, open lanes ahead, lined with pine trees, speckled with cars. I get to the chiro quick enough.

The building is prefab, a glorified doublewide. Metal sheeting for exterior walls. Gravel for the parking lot. The wheelchair ramp crisscrossing up to the front door looks tumorous.

Inside the doublewide it's any generic doctor's office, except one that's trying hard to be someplace else. A lawyer's office, maybe. The living room quality of the lobby is less effective in person. I've waited in worse, but the word cozy doesn't spring to mind. The fake fireplace is too large. The incense overwhelms.

The chiropractor from the commercial meets me at the reception desk and leads me to an examination room. He wears pleated khakis. His goatee is flecked with gray.

Framed posters of famous impressionist paintings festoon the walls. So many waterlilies. The floor is fake wood. Two wingback chairs face each other, dead center. I worry I've come to a shrink by mistake. I sit in the chair on the left, and the chiropractor sits opposite me.

I tell him I'm the guy who made his commercials, and he tells me he's just watched them and they're great and thanks. It seems heartfelt. A rare moment of my job meaning something. Usually, I think of myself as an assembly line.

"So, the body is a system, right." says the chiro.

He doesn't articulate it like a question, so I just stare.

"Right," he says. "The whole thing is interconnected. Your ankle to your arm to your neck and head. And in the center of all that is your spine. That's the piece that does the heavy lifting, if you know what I mean."

I nod absently. That kids' song of bones connected to other bones plays in my brain.

"If the spine is out of whack, then the whole system gets messed up. The electricity flowing through your nerves and muscles gets stuck, and parts of you that are supposed to be able to heal themselves, well, they just can't. They're trying, but your inner energies are blocked. I can see by how you're sitting—don't take this personally, but I'm used to looking at posture—that you've got some misalignment to your spine, and that's definitely behind the headaches you described when you made the appointment."

"Migraines," I say.

"Right, migraines. What we can do for you is open up the energy flow, and basically that allows your body to take care of its own problems. Other doctors want to give you drugs or fancy procedures, when the answer is usually just letting your body heal itself."

I nod again. I'm not sold, a skeptic by nature. But my gesture seems to embolden the chiro, and he launches into more details, more magical powers the body possesses if only we would sit up straight and release them.

He intersperses okay jokes. I polite laugh.

He takes me back to a darkened room for an x-ray.

He leads me to another room full of odd equipment. He has me remove my shirt. I'm embarrassed at the slackness of my body. He rubs some sort of plastic wand on either side of my spine and a computer screen spits out numbers on a bar graph. The chiro emits various mmms and hmmms.

On the way back from the tests, we pass an open room where the blonder, handsomer chiro from the commercial poises over the back of a patient. Think predator over prey. The chiro presses down with both hands. A gross pop like the world's largest knuckle.

We return to the wingback chairs. It turns out one of the impressionist posters on the wall is actually a 50-inch TV. The chiro turns off the poster using an iPad and pulls up grainy x-rays of twisted spines.

"This could be you," he says of a spine that could double as a tree branch.

A lemon scent tinges the room.

The waterlily posters' frames are plastic.

This guy never stops smiling. He's going to need his jawbone adjusted.

He shows me the fucked-up spine of an old man and implies that I, too, will one day be old. He shows me another old man's spine, this one adjusted and straight as lumber. The chiro calls it "lovely." This is several more spines than I've ever scrutinized.

Now it's time for the x-ray of my own spine. It's got unusual twists to it, clear to even my untrained eye.

"See," says the chiropractor, "you're already on the way."

He doesn't explain on the way to what.

He talks about chair design. He says his patients are immune to colds.

It's about now my guts clench. This guy is hocking me my own health like it's a used car. I've edited so many commercials for car dealers.

Go ahead, kick the tires.

I ask about the studies these treatments came from. I ask about peer review.

His glued-on smile falters. The concept of peer review is alien to him. He wouldn't know a medical journal from the *National Enquirer*.

He talks instead about fast food and bowel movements.

A gold cross dangles in the V where his oxford is unbuttoned at the top. I ignore the perfectly manicured line of his goatee.

It's clear he's been trained for this sales pitch. It's too refined, every word calculated. At chiropractor school, he took a 101 course on marketing. He received an A-plus.

I'm queasy even being here.

My pain isn't a used car. It's not a product. I prefer traditional doctors who ignore me over this desperate grab for my business. That's all this guy's after.

Finally come the numbers.

"Your insurance doesn't cover this," he says. His tone implies this is my fault for having shitty insurance.

The massive TV displays the cost for one year of treatment. Almost $9,000, a quarter of my salary. How many used cars could I buy with that?

I fail to contain a chuckle.

"We have payment plans," he says.

"I'm sure you do," I say.

The chiropractor reads my face. It's easy to read.

His smile, his concern, the starch in his shirt, all of it oozes away.

I thank him for his time. My thanks are both lame and a lie.

The chiropractor leaves the room abruptly. Am I supposed to leave, too? I sit there in the wingback. Eventually, a burly man, bouncer material, shows me out with a curt, "This way."

I pass through the lobby. The chiropractor props an elbow on the reception desk. His sleeves are up. Big gold watch. This fucking guy isn't a car salesman, he's a televangelist. I might as well have had a consultation with Preacherman.

I thank him again. What the hell is wrong with me? He barely grunts in response.

I drive away. The metal shack shrinks in my mirrors.

I find a chain restaurant and eat a forgettable lunch. Pooler is 90% chain restaurants.

I choose back roads home. Two lanes lined by pine trees. Old neighborhoods, vintage suburbs.

My back pulls straight. I'm newly aware of my posture. I sense individual vertebrae.

I started the day with a tiny, false hope. That's gone. The loss feels larger than it should. That's the risk of hoping.

No surprise when the aura comes.

I add disappointment to my list of migraine triggers.

October 12

My friends don't respond right away when I text them. That was never the case before. We used to have a group text that buzzed my phone throughout the day. That one, though, went silent when KJ died.

Now, I've got nothing to say except *How are you?* There are only so many answers to that question before a friend runs out.

Where did the damage to my relationships come from?

Is losing more friends a long-term effect of losing one?

Or is it me? Could all be mended if I dredged my ass out of bed early enough for Breakfast Club a couple times a week?

How can I explain the probing pain? When it's bad, it's easy. I hurt to the point I clearly can't be held accountable. But in the interim, when the pain merely threatens, how do you explain the fear?

KJ would have dragged me out to do things. The loss of KJ is likely the reason my remaining friends don't do the same. Our collective will to act died with him. All losses are comorbid.

I'm eroded. Weathered. Diminished. There's less of me than there used to be. To lose all of me now would be insignificant. I'll blow away in a storm.

The sky contains just a few clouds, virgin white.

Every shift I make in my chair echoes in my head. Standing is a risk.

I try to keep my back straight.

I want to sleep. I want the days to pass so I can claim to have survived them.

I don't care if I survive.

Sometimes I drink a rum and Coke and tell myself it's for my headaches when it's really for a different sort of numbness.

I watch TV shows I've watched before so that time blurs. If time is bullshit, then it's all my fault.

I text my friends, *How are you?*

I wait for a reply.

October 21
...

It's Dolores's birthday. We're at Lulu's, a dessert bar on MLK Street. We huddle around a table in the center of the slender room. It's a weeknight, one of those interchangeable evenings, Tuesday-Wednesday-Thursday. Most of the other tables are empty. A few couples on dates. Only two people at the bar, sitting separately.

Dolores has shorn her hair almost down to the scalp, a dusting of black over the skin. Hildie has dyed hers purple. Ollie is unalterable stone.

A glacial slab of chocolate cake masses before Dolores. More than enough for two. But it's hers and hers alone. The fork looks comically small beside it.

The manager, Jill, comes and wishes Dolores *happy birthday*. Jill and I dated before she left town. I knew she'd moved back, but this is the first time I've seen her. I feel a certain sort of flutter. She has a new tattoo on her forearm. I can't tell what it is. Maybe a narwhal? When she visits the table, I glance away.

We promised Dolores not to sing, but I lean close to her and hum the melody. Hildie joins in, and Ollie drops a harmony over top. Ollie is full of surprises.

Dolores attempts her cake. Hildie and Ollie share a saucer of truffles. I have the crème brûlée. KJ used to pronounce it *creamy brew-lee*. I can't even eat dessert without a memory. I crack the top with my spoon.

Blake bustles in, a new guy in tow, though everybody but me knows the new guy already. We make introductions. I'm three Scotches deep and forget the new guy's name immediately. I recall Blake's dates by category. Hair color, build, fashion sense. I add the new guy to the lists for blonds and skinny jeans.

Jill takes Blake and his date's orders. I look out the front window. There's another, busier bar next door. Smokers mingle on the sidewalk. A sooty cloud.

The phosphenes coalesce from the smoke haze. Stars sparking in the universe's primordial dust. I try to name the constellations, but they're fleeting.

Blake gabs happily, buoyantly, and I feed off that, I do. I remember similar nights, feedback loops of fun and friendship and joy.

But what am I to my friends now? Do I offer joy in return?

Hildie smiles at something Blake said. Her mouth stretches wider and wider until she's one-hundred-percent mouth. I think *Cheshire* but my brain can't summon the word *cat*.

The table lengthens. My friends recede. I start to reach out a hand but bump Dolores's martini glass. Only drips left in the bottom. Nothing sloshes.

Jill returns, and she's a giant. The ceiling has been raised to contain her. Her head pierces clouds. She inhales deeply. She used to smoke. I encouraged her to quit. I told myself it was for her health, but it's really because I don't like the smell.

What a shitty boyfriend I am. What a shitty person.

When the pain is on the way, I get so sad. I know I'll have to leave again and disappoint my friends.

Is friendship always a burden? Love, that times two?

I convince myself not to let them down. I brace for the pain.

Another round of drinks. Blake tells a story. My mind is half-lost by this point, so I don't hear exactly what he says, but I can tell the story myself. I was there. It was the night KJ played me in ping pong using only his hand. The way he commentated, the drunken crowd that gathered round to watch.

I worry that a story featuring KJ is the wrong one to share on his fiancé's birthday, but Dolores has a happy-sad expression, grateful for having known, for however long, the thing that now makes you sad.

Blake shares a part of the story I don't remember: before we left the bar, Dolores went and gathered up the dozens of ping pong balls Hildie and Blake had dumped over KJ's head. So a story about KJ, but the punchline is all Dolores.

Lulu's closes, but Jill lets us stay while the staff cleans up. I move from aura to headache. When it's time to go, Jill joins us, and two of the bartenders, too.

We buy a 24-pack of Icehouse at a gas station. Ollie carries the beer like it's a briefcase full of nuclear codes. Hildie leads us into the city. She dances as she walks. I want to dance alongside her. I want to heal enough to want to dance.

I don't dance, not really, not ever.

We end up at the Owenport House, an antebellum mansion-turned-museum on Abercorn Street. A friend who was a docent here showed us a spot where you can sneak into the courtyard. I bend back the sapling concealing the gap and let everybody squeeze through. I check the street for onlookers. I can't see for shit. A lamp flips on in the quaint old townhome across the street.

Spotlights shine up trees in the corners of the courtyard. Pathways meander through a manicured garden. The fountain in the center idles, stagnant.

We sit on the mansion's back steps and pop the tabs on cheap beers. We have hushed conversations. One of the kids who works with Jill lights a joint and passes it around.

There's a lovely time of night when all talk turns to giggles.

I used to know these hours. I used to welcome single digits like old friends.

I sit on the top step. Because I want to see everyone. Because I can't quite participate.

Pain is a burden in the sense of a heavy weight. Every action is taxing.

Jill joins me on the top step. This is a moment from long ago. In a memory, after the bars closed, we'd come here to ride out the night. We were all twenty-somethings then, none of us anymore. Time is bullshit.

Jill says, softly and only to me, "We never maybe said the stuff we should have said."

I nod. I stop nodding when it hurts.

Blue lights strobe on the wall of the building across the street. We all go quiet. Boot-clad footsteps. The yellow cone of a flashlight shines through the metal gate. The light falls on us.

Don't move, says one of the cops, or some cliché like that. But we're up. We abandon our empty cans, which seems inconsiderate. The joint smolders on a step. We go out to the secret way in. We scatter to the night, sprinting each in our own direction.

A bursting firework.

A dropped palmful of ping pong balls.

I make it half a block before the pain throbs too hard to continue. It knocks me to a knee. Then Dolores is there helping me up. We walk arm in arm. When the cops drive by, they ask if we saw anybody running. We tell them *yeah* and point the wrong way.

We catch up with Jill on the next block.

She inspects my face with concern. She asks if I'm okay. I try to answer but the words lodge in my brain. Dolores explains the migraines for me.

"I thought something was off earlier," Jill says.

I offer to walk Dolores home, but she calls for a ride. We wait with her.

"I appreciate you sticking it out with a migraine," Dolores says.

"Happy birthday," I say.

"It's already tomorrow."

Her ride comes. It's just me and Jill and the morning.

October 22

Jill came home with me. We didn't do anything except guzzle cups of water and get in bed. She stroked my hair, hypnotizing away the pain until I fell asleep. It's nearly noon when we wake.

We straighten ourselves up and head down to the coffee shop. We pick up coffee and croissants to go. There's a chill in the air, the first of the season. Not outright cold yet, so everyone is taking Sunday brunches. Fewer tourists in fall.

Jill fills me in on the gap from when we were an *us* until now. I know some of it, of course. I knew when she left where she was going. Her dream of being a screenwriter. I saw online what she's done since then, whether I was trying to see it or not. Usually, I was trying.

"I murdered myself in New York," she says, "and LA wasn't any easier. And you see the ratio, who makes it to who doesn't, and I swear you're just as likely to sell a screenplay living anywhere else. Maybe not. Maybe I'm a quitter. But I'd rather my remaining decades, the everyday of them, mean more. If the big chance comes, then I can always go back to LA. Until then, I want to be with people I like in the place that feels like home."

I should object that it's unwise to expect decades. Grab the big moments while you can because one day, you're dead and poof, game over.

We ride the silence for a block.

"So," she says, "about the stuff we never said."

"You were on the way to a new life. I think we were avoiding the burden of what saying those things would mean."

Several more blocks.

"I'm sorry to hear about the migraines," she says. "Chronic illness is such shit to deal with."

I stop walking. A man fat with brunch bumps past me and mutters rudenesses.

"You okay?" asks Jill.

Chronic illness. It's been over half a year, and I've never once thought of my condition as chronic. I've treated it instead like the extended cut of a hangover.

"Sorry," I say.

We start walking again. We round the corner and pass our favorite Mexican restaurant. We wander down Broughton Street. Pedestrians haul shopping bags, come and go from storefronts. Their actions are mechanical. A clockwork city.

I think of the decades ahead. How many years of pain will I accumulate?

We hug and part at Bull Street. Jill rents an apartment in the middle of the historic district. I don't ask her how she affords it. I saw online that she'd managed to sell at least a couple of her projects.

"Number's the same," she says.

I give her a thumbs up. I hate myself for the gesture as I make it. Awkwardness is chronic, too.

I head home. I'm hungover. That twins with the aftereffects of the migraine.

My sense of the future is fucked, stretched out one moment, truncated the next. Time is bullshit, I should have told her. Not with spite, but with care. A heads up. A warning.

I'd call Jill, I would. But I'm not sure I have the decades left she's asking for.

And besides, the hurt has turned me into someone other than the person she remembers.

October 27
...

Philosopher Valerie Gray Hardcastle in *The Myth of Pain*: "For chronic pain, some combination of methods is generally used, for no one method works alone. Combinations of methods rarely work either, however."

Well, fuck.

November 2

In Joan Didion's one short essay on her chronic migraines, she writes, "That no one dies of migraine seems, to someone deep into an attack, an ambiguous blessing."

As if blessings come any other way.

November 4
...

My neurologist appointment is across town. I drive a road with actual traffic to get there. Miles of six lanes lined with shopping strips. As soon as you leave downtown, Savannah transforms into anywhere else.

Gripping the wheel, I'm extra aware of the muscles in my shoulders. They tug at other muscles in my arms and back and neck. A body is a system, the chiro said. That much I abide. Pulleys and weights.

I turn off the main strip. I pass the hospital where KJ was pronounced DOA. Where I was brought after the anaphylaxis. My head fuzzes at the sight of the entrance. My front tire rubs the curb.

The road circles the hospital. I complete three orbits before I finally pull into the neuro's parking lot.

I make good time, even with the orbits. Too early to go in, even with new-patient paperwork.

I find a picnic table under an oak tree. It's chilly, but an outside chill is preferable to a waiting-room chill.

A squirrel hops up on the table, tame as can be. I wonder who around here feeds her. She's obviously pregnant, the squirrel. Not that I'm an expert in what pregnant squirrels look like. I chat with the squirrel, and the sweet creature sits there and takes it.

I tell my friend the squirrel goodbye and enter the office.

The receptionist gives me a clipboard full of papers that have obviously been copied from copies from other copies for generations. I sign my name on the bottom of every page that asks for it. I have no idea what I'm signing.

I read a gloss-faded copy of *Sports Illustrated*. I'm less worried about germs at the neuro than I am at my regular doctor's office. People here are a different kind of sick.

The magazine recaps the baseball season. The whole season has passed without me noticing.

I'm called back. When I put the magazine down, I notice another magazine I would've rather read. I follow the nurse through flickering corridors.

"I sat outside before I came in," I tell him. "A squirrel hopped up on the picnic table with me."

"They're pretty tame around here," he says. "People always feeding them."

"The squirrel looked pregnant."

"Oh!" His expression shifts to interested. "That's Matilda. She's the friendliest of the bunch."

"That's a great name for a squirrel," I say.

The nurse deposits me in an examination room. I note what's different here versus at my regular doc, but every detail is the same.

I've got no headache today. Sure, there's the twinge where one might come, but for once I'm not scared of it. I'm here for a cure, after all.

I enter doctor time. Each moment stretches.

Quick, take my pulse, it'll be so slow and healthy.

The neurologist enters, and I note two facts right away: he is kind, and he is old. I'm happy for the former, the way kindness is creased in the corners of his eyes. The latter is clear from his thick, arthritic knuckles. His fingers curl like talons.

He introduces himself and reads my chart. My life is so well documented these days. He makes just-audible hums for my benefit, noises of appraisal.

"A migraineur," he says, more to the room than to me. "Sorry, you don't mind that term, do you? It's dated. We're not really supposed to use it now."

"I don't mind," I say. I've seen the term on the internet.

"I understand the change in terminology," he says. "You don't want to confuse the patient for the condition. You don't want them to be forced to identify themselves as the thing that hurts them."

"Isn't that what everybody does, anyway?"

He speaks a *ha*. "I see we've got a philosopher here."

I look down at the floor. The tiles are a noncolor between beige and gray.

"How about your migraine diary?" he asks. "Have you kept it up? Learned anything from it?"

"Nothing particularly useful."

"That's how it goes a lot of the time, sadly."

The doctor flips the pages of the chart back and forth.

"An NSAID allergy. And hospitalized for it. In a way you're lucky about the hospitalization. Usually when that's listed in somebody's file, my first thought is they're after pain pills. Especially a skinny guy like you, no offense. I try not to be jaded in this job, and I don't fault anyone with an addiction, but I've seen it all so often. It's best to have the allergy documented. It'll keep doctors from balking if you ever need stronger medicine for pain."

He flips back to the front of my chart and tosses it on the counter. The metal clipboard clatters.

"I'll give you an exam now," he says, "because that's what I'm supposed to do. Before I start, though, I want to be clear that I think I already know what I'm going to tell you, and I also know it's not going to be what you want to hear."

"Thanks?" I say.

He smiles. His teeth are coffee stained.

He checks my reflexes. He checks my heartbeat. He shines a penlight into my eye and then away, into the other eye and away. I'm impressed with how well he does all this with arthritic hands.

He asks generic questions about diet and exercise. He asks about specifics from my migraine diary, nodding absently at my answers. He never adds any notes to my chart.

"It's good news, bad news time," he says. "I'm confident this is a standard migraine situation. I'm not worried that there might be anything dangerously wrong with your brain. Migraines are awful but benign.

"As far as treatment, your GP was right. You don't have full-blown migraines often enough to justify the risks of more aggressive treatment. If you were laid up with migraines every other day or more, then we could talk, but for now you're getting by, and that's sometimes the best we can offer a migraineur."

His face slackens. His wrinkles sag. The veil of doctor slips away.

"Look," he says. "I've been doing this for forty years. There've been advancements in so many areas, but we still don't understand migraines. We know them better, sure, but there's no cure. We manage them, that's all. And a lot of what we've done to manage them has turned out to be wrong. Even Botox, which works well for some people, often stops working after a while. I worry everything we do is just placebo. That's maybe why some patients have success with alternative treatments. Chiropractors and acupuncture and the like. I doubt those make a real difference, but I've had patients benefit from them, and that's the goal, isn't it?"

"I'm not much for chiropractors," I say.

He grabs my chart and a notepad from the counter and scrawls two words.

"I'm recommending a pair of nutraceuticals. These are things you can find in the vitamin aisle at the drugstore. Riboflavin and magnesium. They've both been tested to reduce migraine frequency and headache duration, but to be honest, I've never had a patient say they made much of a difference. Hope springs eternal, though, right?"

He tears the top page off the pad and hands it to me. The corner of the page is ripped, a jagged angle. The doctor clicks his pen shut and taps the tip on my chart.

"I have one last question. In the notes your GP sent over, it mentions that the initial onset of symptoms happened at a friend's funeral?"

"Yeah," I say.

"Do you experience depression?"

I shrug.

"That's not my area, so I won't diagnose you, but I'm adding a note. It might be worth considering psychiatric care."

"I have migraines because I'm sad?"

"And you're sad because you have migraines. The conditions can be related. Again, I'm not promising you any cure, but we want to get you feeling as right as possible using whatever techniques we have at our disposal."

I focus on the word *disposal*.

The doctor thanks me and I thank him.

The world is so goddamn grateful.

I'm left alone in the room to wait. White walls, drop ceiling, paper-topped examination table, boring tile, posters illustrating various neurological ailments. Every detail familiar.

I like the neuro, I really do, but I vow no more doctors. No more waiting rooms. No more copays.

Am I sad? Of course I'm sad. Who isn't? Who can be other than sad, other than pained, other than in proximity to death?

A migraine aura starts on my drive home. Of course, it happens as soon as I've left the person I'd want to observe its effects. The cars on the road stretch into limousines. The stoplights facet and sparkle and radiate. I pull into a Buffalo Wild Wing parking lot until the blindness subsides. I wait for the hurt.

At home I sit on the couch. Instead of trying to hide from the pain, I make myself experience it full-on. I embrace each throb. I resign myself.

I'm wrecked, but not just by the migraine. It's the cycle of hope and resignation. The fact that after every visit to every doctor I tell myself *enough* only to schedule the next appointment.

I pull the note with the nutraceuticals from my pocket and shred the paper as fine as my fingers can manage. I let the strips fall to the floor. No more false hopes, I tell myself.

But I know the thing with cycles is that they come around again.

November 6
...

For migraine patients, "what one may have to remedy, if it can be remedied, is a whole way of life, a whole life." So says Oliver Sacks, who wrote the book on migraines, literally.
But what's the remedy for life?
I don't want to follow that line of thought. Not yet.

November 15

I dig my thumbnail into my forearm. I stop just short of breaking the skin.

The sting is sweet. I taste the sweetness in my mouth like store-brand mouthwash.

I make six indented crescents, one for each month since KJ died.

The marks fade, but the pain remains.

This pain feels somehow right. I can control it. I can decide its depth and its extent and its very existence.

Jill texted today. We message back and forth. It feels good to communicate, but I don't want to force a chronic condition on someone else. We never schedule a date.

A scratch, even a small one, contains all the elements of a larger pain. It triggers the same nerves, the same impulses. A welt is the same inflammation as with a twisted ankle. The initial sting gives way to the same lingering ache.

How, then, are these two pains entirely different? Why does one wreck me when the other merely annoys? Why is one a pain and the other the hurt?

Hurt seems too small a word, but it's the only word I've got.

November 18

I pry open my eyes and know it's KJ's birthday. The knowledge smacks me, a divine revelation. There's also pain, a full migraine upon waking. Knowledge can be a kind of pain, too.

I struggle to the kitchen and make a rum and Coke. I make it too strong. I chug it down, anyway. I make another and tell myself I'm sipping, but it's gone as fast as the first.

I go to the bathroom to get a triptan. The plastic packaging weighs tons. The childproof bubble is too much for me. I open the thing after the dozenth try. I cup water from my palm to my mouth and swallow the pill.

My heartbeats jackhammer the spot behind my eye. The drinks and the pill clog my esophagus. I swallow hard three times. The fluid dislodges. I will peristalsis. I don't think I'll puke.

I cry, though. The tears leave sticky slug trails on my face. A kaleidoscopic wormhole opens. I fall forward through it. The sound of a vortex. Electrical zaps. I travel across the universe and end up back on my couch.

KJ stands in front of me. I'm so happy he's here, that I can wish him happy birthday to his face. Life can finally revert to normal. But his face is wrong. It's set in rictus. The white of his left eye is bloody red, his iris faded to gray. His limbs are swollen, belly distended. Flesh rots. Orifices writhe with maggots.

The hurt is so severe. It transcends. Worse than any pain I've ever experienced. Not broken bones, not surgery. I weep, and I can't pinpoint the cause.

There's no proper diagnosis for tears.

Whenever I dare open my eyes, KJ's there. I beg him to leave. After only wanting him back, yearning for his return, willing to trade anything, I can't stand the sight of him like this.

The hurt is screaming, and my mind is screaming, a constant onslaught.

This is what KJ felt when he died. He's here now to take me with him.

I dial 9 and 1 on my phone but don't finish.

I conjure a half-lucid thought: there's only one possible end to a chronic illness.

Back in the bathroom, I remove the ibuprofen from the medicine cabinet. My vision is blurry, and I can't read the label, but it's the biggest bottle by far. I never trashed it. It's been there the whole time, a warning I see every day. An invitation.

I dump tablets into my hand. Too many to count. They're round and brown, a palmful of rabbit turds. The image turns my stomach. My stomach is already turned. I forget where I am. I remember. I bring the tablets to my mouth and swallow them all down.

I wait for what happens. I wait for death to claim me. Eons pass, but it's really only seconds. Time and space are bullshit.

I'm sitting on the bathroom floor, face pressed against the toilet. Some sober part of my brain intervenes. Some dormant instinct awakes.

I hoist myself up by the lip of the sink. The medicine cabinet is still open, the mirror angled away from me. I grab at the objects inside, scattering them across the bathroom. I find my toothbrush and flop back to the floor. I jab the brush into my throat. The wretch is feral, a violent spasm. A muscle pulls in my back. Again with the toothbrush. Up come the pills and booze and bile. Vomiting makes my head feel like it's going to erupt.

I don't know if I get it all out. The pills are no longer in a condition to count them. I didn't count them in the first place.

There's a package of allergy medicine on the floor beside me, spilled from the medicine cabinet. I struggle a pill free from the foil-backed package. I swallow it down with a mouthful of spit. I track the pill's path through my body. My insides are scraped and lacerated.

I text Hildie: I need help. Please come.

I drag myself out of the bathroom. Still on the floor, though, leaning on the sofa. Hildie knocks. How much time has passed? I push my hands into the grain of the parquet, but I don't have the strength to stand. She opens the door. I must have left it unlocked. I take this as the first good sign in months.

Hildie sits on the floor next to me. I explain what happened. What I did. She pulls out her phone to call an ambulance, but I stop her.

"Please," I say. "Just you. I'm ok. I just need to know somebody's here to keep an eye on me."

"You sure you puked it all up?"

"I can't puke anymore, if that's what you're asking."

She grins at me. I'm gladdened by my own joke.

I climb onto the couch with Hildie's help. She props me up with pillows. I start to drift off, but startle awake in a small panic.

"Don't tell Dolores," I say. "Please."

"I wouldn't dream of it."

"It hurts so bad."

"Call me first, okay?"

"I promise."

Sleep comes. Not deep. The pain won't allow that.

Whenever I drift toward consciousness, Hildie's with me. There's a lesson in that, but my mind is too broken to learn it.

DIARY THREE

November 19
...

I've been depressed before. Hell, I've been depressed *often*. I've harbored dark thoughts, terminal thoughts. Hopelessness and self-loathing. But I never knew suicide could be a sudden decision. I thought it was an act that had to be built up to. The culmination of a process.

But what is it they say on cop shows, *motive and opportunity*? Perhaps the impulse has been there all along.

Pain is a constant reminder you're alive. I think sometimes we need to forget. We need to remain unaware of our physical selves to keep on living. It doesn't pay to stare at the absurd fact that we're bodies, sentient for one short beat of history.

Hildie straightened my bathroom, returned pill bottles and toothpaste and cotton swabs to the medicine cabinet. Not the ibuprofen, though. That bottle is gone. The trashcan has been emptied.

Did she take the bottle to prevent me from trying something again or to keep me from being reminded of what I almost did?

Motivations, like causes, are rarely clear-cut, anyway.

November 24

...

Audre Lorde writes, "I must let this pain flow through me and pass on. If I try to stop it, it will detonate inside me, shatter me, splatter my pieces against every wall and person that I touch."

I feel bad comparing my condition to her cancer. Migraines are benign, the neurologist said. But pain is never benign.

Pain wounds. Pain inflicts. Pain harms.

Do I have the strength to become the conduit Lorde calls for?

Maybe it's a skill that can be learned. Sure, the practice colossally sucks, but you can get better at a bad thing. Can't you?

I hope.

December 10

I've been to Breakfast Club every day this week. I've cut back on coffee, though. A single cup. I had to train Chris not to bring refills automatically.

Less coffee, fewer headaches. Are the two related? I look back through these diaries to see if there's a correlation, but the only answer I find is *maybe*. I've been looking for a cause long enough to learn that causes are obscure. There are no pinpoints in a blur.

But the endless feeling of impending migraine has broken. The migraines come, but now I can barter with the hurt in exchange for a life. I can claim the gaps in my chronic condition.

Will this last?

What does?

Today, Ollie's off on his latest military assignment. I'm only vaguely aware of what he does when he's not here. I suppose we need blank parts of our friends, some potential to get to know them more.

In Ollie's usual spot, on the other side of Hildie, sits Jill. She's becoming the person I text most often. We talk at night until one of us falls asleep with our phones on. Sometimes when we talk, I'm transported back to a time before all that's happened, happened. If not transported, then reconnected.

I don't know where all this is going, but it feels good to be going somewhere.

December 30

Headache Day. When I have a migraine come on, that's what I text Dolores, Hildie, and Jill. Just to let them know.

I take a triptan, for what it's worth.

The corgi emerges from the paper without fanfare. I follow him outside and through downtown onto Islands Expressway. The trees on either side of the road coalesce into a solid green wall. We emerge into open marsh. The sky is highlighter blue. The road is a pencil mark ahead of us.

Diamond-shaped signs alert us to crossing tortoises. There are so many tortoises, endless queues of them. We're in a video game where you're supposed to avoid running the tortoises over. They're so slow. The game is extra easy.

Tybee Lighthouse rises over the island, the spinning beam like a laser. The water tower on the other end of the island is painted a shade of blue that in no way matches the sky.

We cross the footbridge over the dunes to North Beach. The corgi carries a plastic pail, the kind kids get for cheap from beach shops. He sits in the soft sand above the high-water mark. The sand isn't quite white but might as well be in the sun.

I face the ocean. The water wiggles like gelatin.

Baby sea turtles skitter all around us. There are a million of them. A green-black, ambling wave, cresting in the wrong direction. I compare their motion to that of the tortoises. Flippers versus feet. No clear advantage to either.

I remember watching a nature documentary about how many of the baby turtles will die straight away.

"Good luck," I say to the baby turtles.

"As if luck has shit to do with it," says the corgi in KJ's voice.

He takes a plastic spade from the bucket and shovels sand into a perfect little mountain. The sand is silver, glittering. He exchanges the spade for pair of tweezers. He pincers individual grains, one at a time, onto his mountain's peak.

"Wanna, like, go do something?" I ask.

"I *am* doing something," he says.

I count the grains as he drops them, but numbers aren't working for me. Anyway, after a point, the only number is *a lot*. Days pass this way. The sun rises over the water again and again and again. The little mountain is unchanging.

If someone asked for a demonstration of futility, this might be it.

The sky swarms with seagulls. They fly in firework patterns. They eddy and swirl. Their wings slice at the air.

The gulls disperse, fog-like. Where they'd been, gray clouds. The clouds part. The sun is brighter than it's ever been, pure white. It lasers rays from straight overhead.

I remember nonspecific facts about Egyptian pyramids and astronomy.

The corgi tweezes another grain, lifting it as if in offering to the sun. The grain scintillates. A spark or a star or a phosphene. He adds it to his mountain.

Sand avalanches down one side.

The shift is only inches.

The corgi pulls an egg salad sandwich out of the pail. He talks between smacking mouthfuls.

"You spend a lot of time looking for reasons, but I don't think you realize how reasons work. You want to say that last grain of sand triggered the change. You want to point to this single, specific cause, but that means ignoring the whole chain of events leading up to it. How many grains of sand did there have to be before the last one could do its thing? I'm not talking bullshit and butterfly wings." The corgi finishes the sandwich and opens a bag of potato chips. Crumbs fall out of his mouth as he talks. "Eventually, after enough small changes, a big change comes. That's life. That's the universe. The problem with being a self-aware asshole in a chaotic universe is that sometimes the big change colossally sucks."

He offers me a chip, but I decline. I won't be able to taste it. My tongue is numb. He finishes the chips and crinkles the bag into the pail.

People start coming over the walkway. Dozens of them, then hundreds. Happy beachgoers. Their flip-flops tap out a rhythm on the footbridge.

It's such a fine sunny day, summertime.

I try to remember the actual time of year, for what it's worth.

The corgi wades into the ocean. I fret his ink will dissolve, but he swims around, no worries. Porpoises cavort in a circle around him. They leap from the water and re-break the surface with barely a splash.

Everyone on the beach sways to the beat of a song I can't hear.

All this choreography is too goddamn much.

"Find it," says the corgi.

He waves. It's a goodbye wave.

The sun brightens, washing out the world.

I'm back in my room. Nighttime.

The corgi rests two-dimensional on his sheet of paper.

A quick sketch. A gift from my oldest friend.

January 1
...

On her years of debilitating illness, author Sarah Manguso reflects, "Nothing happens in a moment. Nothing happens quickly. If you think something's happened quickly, you're only looking at a part of it."

We overvalue what we believe to be the final step.

We let the most obvious moment eclipse everything else.

But spacetime is a continuum. We're always somewhere in the middle, as much ahead of us as behind.

I like the implication of that.

I like that there's no difference between progressing and pausing just to breathe.

January 27
...

Jill and I stroll after dinner, killing time. There's an opalescent sheen to the surface of the world like sometimes happens in winter. My fingertips are numb, but it's just from the cold.

We're passing the apartments next to mine, a mid-century building, all concrete and glass. The only structure of that era downtown. Jill halts me with a tug on my hand. She punches a code into a keypad by the front door. The machinery of the door whirs, then a click.

This is odd in that Jill doesn't live here. As far as I know, nobody does. They started a renovation, gutting the place, but it's stayed empty. Through the windows all you can see is raw space.

The lobby has been refurbished, at least. It's almost posh.

I ask Jill how she got the code.

"When I moved back, I came to an open house. Practically giving away square footage. I mean, you'd have to hire a contractor to build out the interior. Anyway," she flicks a thumb at the keypad, "I peeked over the realtor's shoulder."

We board the elevator, glossy like the lobby but dusted over from disuse. Jill hits the button for the tenth floor. There are eleven floors total. The elevator shrugs from still and then rises smoothly.

The tenth floor is dusk-lit from outside, windows in all directions, the entire exterior wall. Where would you hang a painting? Where would you change clothes? Bare concrete for the floor, the ceiling, the columns. Wires dangle and sway all over, jungle vines.

Our footsteps echo. I navigate like a bat. Old odors smear with the fresher dust of the renovation.

We tiptoe to the windows. We're eyelevel with the cathedral's spires. We make a lap of the place, pausing to point out new angles of familiar sights.

Our voices sound small. We hold hands and release when our palms get sweaty and hold hands again when the sweat dries.

I catalog each moment. This is a memory that will carry meaning later. I've traveled forward in time to the place where I'm remembering. I flash back to the night the photo was taken of me and Jill watching fireworks. How many years ago was that?

Time and space are bullshit.

The elevator dings. I startle and release a humiliating yelp. Jill and I duck behind a column. The elevator doors slide open, but it's empty inside. A brassy glow. A ghost, maybe, telling us it's time to leave. The elevator doors pinch shut.

"Did you just—yip?" asks Jill.

I can't deny it, so I kiss her. We share a single accelerated heart. It's all so ridiculous, isn't it? Being happy and being scared and being relieved.

We meet Dolores, Hildie, and Ollie at Pinkie's. They're already in the big booth by the door. Blake's at the bar with a new guy. Lyn and Pru and Chuck sit together over in another booth. People we know but know less well stand in the corner. We say hello to everyone, to the whole grand goddamn world.

At one point in the evening, a man comes over to Dolores and chats her up. I've seen him around before, but we've never spoken. He runs in our circles, but not the inner one. I watch Dolores while pretending I'm not. I'm well on drunk. I suspect I'm obvious.

She's laughing with the man and smiling, and god, I'd forgotten the impact of her happiness, the whole city made brighter by it. One more memory to save from this night.

The man leaves. It was more than a friendly chat but not much more. Not yet.

He's got a cute butt, I note as he walks to the bar. I nod to myself about it. Dolores sees me and turns bashful. I squeeze her hand. The cold around her melts away, an aura I only now notice as it goes.

More drinks and more friends and more conversations. We're outside at some point, the five of us, making a riot on quiet residential streets. Big-ass townhomes hunker darkened around us. Millionaires asleep within. KJ once said, "If you can't piss on the rich, at least you can piss them off."

I remember remembering him.

I remember thinking about streetlights and the black branches of trees. My memory turns fuzzy here. All that's left is the sensation of warmth on a chilly night.

Anyway, how do you write about a blur?

February 5
...

In her memoir, *Head Case*, Lex Orgera writes: "The truth is, it was just another migraine, and migraine comes and goes for a grab bag of reasons."

Maybe that's the hard part to stomach, that I have fewer migraines now, but I'll never understand why.

None of it makes sense. It *resists* sense.

Pain can't be a story. Pain punctuates, never arcs. It comes in wave after wave.

I flip through the blank pages ahead of me. Will I fill them?

What's the point of writing about this anyway?

Connecting dots with imaginary lines.

The thing with constellations is that the shapes are all in our heads.

Is it a joke to say that about a migraine?

My Personal History of Pain
Part VI
...

Ten years ago, new to the city, sitting at a table in Gallery Espresso because I got it in my head that's how friends were made, simply by being in public. I didn't live downtown yet, so at the end of an evening of sitting alone, maybe after a drink at the pub across the street, I'd drive home. All my thoughts would collapse around me, loneliness coupling with adriftness, and the imbalanced chemicals in my brain would absolutely scream hateful slurs, and my face would feel misshapen, distorted by causeless grief, and I'd be crying, my foot stomping the accelerator, hands twitching on the wheel in the direction of a bridge abutment, the clear solution in my cloudy mind to silence the screaming of it all.

But that's not how that old inner hurt stopped. I didn't have the means or the will to take care of it myself.

One evening, writing in a notebook, a novel splayed open on the table next to it—I can't recall the novel, and it seems an important piece of information now lost—I was interrupted by a clearing of the throat and a friendly, "Hey."

KJ stood beside my table. I didn't know him yet, but he was at the coffee shop a lot, a face I recognized. I knew so many faces but so few voices.

"Mind if I sit," he said, already placing his black Jansport on the chair across from me.

The rest of the coffee shop was full, every seat occupied. The air filled with a blur of chatter, the burnt scent of too much coffee.

The table wobbled as he pulled things from his bag and arranged them: a sketch pad, a pencil case, a Justice League comic book with Metamorpho on the cover, a superhero I'd only learn to identify later.

"I'm KJ," he said.

How could I know then that four-letter sentence was the first dose of a cure?

We talked from there, neither of us working on the stuff spread out on the table. I'd forgotten what it was like to talk at length, to string words aloud into sentences and sentences into thoughts.

What did we talk about? Ten years is too long ago to recall. I can remember scraps of old conversations, but those could have been from any night. The joy of a long friendship lies somewhere in the misremembering. The blurring.

Eventually, we settled in to work. I wrote the first paragraphs of what would become my first published story. KJ worked on sketches for a comic book he was developing. He'd never finish it. He was great at getting started but rarely pushed big projects through to completion. He always held more ideas inside than a single person could contain. He always moved on to the next thing.

At the table beside us, a pair of loud talkers overshared about their recent failed relationships. KJ sketched them in rough, boisterous linework. Their eyes and mouths frantic with energy even in the frozen image. The speech bubble between them was filled with gibberish, the types of symbols usually reserved for profanity, a black scribble over that. KJ gave the sketch to me, his grin fierce. I would learn he loved nothing more than observing people in exposed moments.

Maybe he recognized a similar exposure in me.

Sometimes I doubt this memory, the swirling shape of the room superimposed from other nights, memory stacked upon memory stacked upon memory. Maybe there were other tables open. Maybe he saw me exposed and decided that's where he should be.

Fuck fate. It feels better to have been chosen.

That first sketch is in a file folder in a box in my closet, sandwiched with the others from KJ I had the wherewithal to save.

KJ started to pack up his stuff. The shock of pending aloneness stilled my own writing. I felt better, yes, but after only one dose of the medicine that healed my tired mind, the fear of the return of the hurt was as bad as the hurt itself. You can't remember pain, but of course you can.

"I'm heading over to Pinkie's," he said.

It was a statement, not an invitation exactly. I was faced with two possible answers: "Cool," a dismissal, or "I'm game," an acceptance. Sometimes I think my whole life hinged on working up the courage for the latter. I packed up, too, and we left, and the night was just getting started.

That first evening would become every evening that week, and then most evenings for weeks and months. How often do you find, by chance in a crowded room, a friendship that can only be cut short, in the end, by death?

I wonder now if what worried me most when KJ died was a return to my life from before. But there are two types of cures: the ones that treat the symptoms and the ones that treat the cause.

I think I'll be alright, migraines notwithstanding.

Sometimes the cure is simply in learning how to cope.

March 13, one year later

...

No one articulates the plan to come to Tybee. Hildie says, *Let's go for a ride,* and Dolores and I climb into her ratty Civic hatchback. The backseat is mine alone.

Hildie steers us toward the islands. We breeze over Whitmarsh, Talahi, and Wilmington. The long stretch through the marsh. Low tide. Trickles of water break up muddy islands, capped with marsh grass.

The parking lot by the lighthouse is half full. Every outdoor table at North Beach Grill is taken. It's a nice day, I realize. Not quite beach weather, but close.

We cross the footbridge over the dunes. The planks thump with our steps. The ocean air whips us, salty, a whiff of sulfur from the mouth of the river.

Clouds wisp overhead, thin like gauze, almost not clouds at all.

The waves loom taller and taller the farther out you look. Giant container ships steam into port. There are always a few ships on the horizon.

Sand kicks up into my shoe and rubs the flesh raw on my ankle. None of us dressed for the beach. It's cooler in the wind off the water. I hug myself and wish for a jacket.

We stop at the approximate spot where we left our friend. Deposited. Buried. There's no right word for it. By this point, KJ's been carried who knows where. The waves lap up and pull back. I watch long enough to guess the tide is ebbing.

Hildie has a driftwood stick, drawing patterns in the damp sand.

I check on Dolores. She's not crying. She's not smiling. Some state between the two. She scatters a cluster of shells with her toe.

This beach is just a beach again. I harbor the selfish hope that we'll return soon with towels and books and beers. We'll spend whole days in the sun.

There's a pain behind my left eye, but the soft kind, the kind that usually doesn't get worse.

My head is full of such strange categories.

I haven't figured out for sure what KJ's corgi wanted me to find, but I think the real KJ would tell me this: go do things, even when it hurts, because nothing else is life.

ACKNOWLEDGMENTS

Thanks to Amy Freeman, Catherine Killingsworth, Hannah Grieco, and Annie Bomke for giving the manuscript an early read. Thanks to Amber Sparks for taking the time to talk to me about migraines. Thanks to my early readers/blurbers, Jose Hernandez Diaz and Patricia Lockwood.

Thanks to everyone at JackLeg Press, especially Jennifer Harris, Erik Noonan, and Matt Dube, and to my publicist, Penina Roth. Thanks to Christopher Kardambikis for the cover art, Emily Fussner Lam for the cover design, and Tiffany Lueong for the author photo.

Thanks to everyone at The Writer's Center, especially my colleagues over the years: Emily Holland, Laura Spencer, Margaret Meleney, Brandon Johnson (Blue), Claude Olson, Manuela Galindo, Grace Mott, Woody Woodger, and everybody else. Thanks to the board, our instructors, and all the other writers this rad job has let me come to know.

Thanks to old friends who've snuck their first names into this book: Christopher Berinato, Blake "Allfather" Patrick, Alison Niebanck, and Matt Garappolo. And to the too-many-to-list other friends who shared some of the real places and experiences that inspired my made-up scenes.

Thanks to the writers whose work I reference: Anne Boyer, Marcelo Hernandez Castillo, Joan Didion, William Dunbar translated by Jenni Nuttall, Valerie Gray Hardcastle, Porochista Khakpour, Audre Lorde, Sarah Manguso, Maggie Nelson, Lex Orgera, Oliver Sacks, Elaine Scarry, Patrick Wall, Esmé Weijun Wang, Ludwig Wittgenstein, and Virginia Woolf.

Thanks to Dr. Seth fdor recommending the first drug to actually help me manage my migraines.

In memory of Kirk Lawrence and Jeremy Mullins, who more than anyone helped me lay the foundation for living a creative life. I hope I've managed to make some art you'd like.

Thanks to my family, as always!

Thanks and love to Stephanie Grimm and ShyCat and Chernushka and Kirby!

JackLeg Press Authors
jacklegpress.org

V. Joshua Adams
Mark Baumgartner
Gayle Brandeis
Scott Shibuya Brown
Michael Chin
Chloe Clark
Rivka Clifton
Brittney Corrigan
Jessica Cuello
Barbara Cully
Allison Cundiff
Curious Theatre Branch
Neil de la Flor
Genevieve DeGuzman
Suzanne Frischkorn
Victoria Garza
Reginald Gibbons
Joachim Glage
Caroline Goodwin
Brett Hanley
Summer Hart
Kathryn Kruse

Brigitte Lewis
Jenny Magnus
DK McCutchen
Jean McGarry
Rita Mookerjee
Mamie Morgan
Beau O'Reilly
Lex Orgera
Zach Powers
Karen Rigby
Jo Salas
Maureen Seaton
Kristine Snodgrass
Cornelia Spelman
Peter Stenson
Melissa Studdard
Jennifer Tseng
Gemini Wahhaj
Megan Weiler
David Welch
Cassandra Whitaker
David Wesley Williams

www.ingramcontent.com/pod-product-compliance
Lightning Source LLC
LaVergne TN
LVHW040051080526
838202LV00045B/3584